KW-328-577

*The Wehrmacht series by Horst Weitzer translated by
George Hirst available from New English Library:*

PANZERGRENADIER
GENOCIDE AT ST-HONOR

GENOCIDE AT ST-HONOR

Horst Weitzer

translated by George Hirst

NEW ENGLISH LIBRARY

NEL Books are published by
New English Library,
Barnard's inn, Holborn,
London, EC1N 2JR, a division of Hodder and Stoughton Ltd.

Printed and bound in Great Britain by
©ollins, Glasgow

0 450 05275 3

Chapter One

The second rifle shot rang out within a split-second of the first. The two were so close that their echoes converged into a single blast which shattered the peace of the summer night.

And with those shots young Hansruedi Wiederkehr, who had served in France for less than a week and Gottfried Brodmann, who was old enough to have been Wiederkehr's grandfather, both died instantly with bullets through their hearts.

Neither of them had a chance to realise what was happening. They had been leaning over the stone parapet of the fourteenth-century west bridge in the French village of Talmont-les-deux-Ponts and chatting animatedly about a town on the Eder not far from Siegen which they both knew well. This was a holiday place where, before the war, young Wiederkehr had spent three summers with his parents. It was also the heaven where Brodmann had shared his honeymoon thirty-three years ago with his bride, Sieglinda Schmitt. "Ziggy" he'd always called her.

Now the two Wehrmacht infantrymen were dead and the night was quiet again. Beneath the ancient bridge the river Loze, a small tributary to the mighty Loire, glided on unperturbed between deep banks bordered by tall elms, willows and alders; small eddies in the current threaded by the half-moon into a silver mosaic.

Armand Guerineau, commanding the Loze detachment of the French Communist-inspired Resistance group Franc Tireurs et Partisans, nodded curtly towards the man standing beside him holding the German G-41 (M) 7·92mm sniper's rifle. He knew there had been little chance of Guy Simon missing such sitting targets. "Kill-a-Boche-a-day!" was Simon's maxim. He'd be well satisfied! He'd got two of the bastards already and it was only one-thirty in the morning.

The two Frenchmen remained in cover at the corner of Pouroux's *boulangerie* where the road was screened in shadow, their eyes fixed on the bridge on the chance that other

Wehrmacht guards might have reacted to the shooting and were racing to investigate. But there were no sounds of running soldiers. If the Boches had heard, then they must have turned over in their sleep and gone on with their snoring.

This was a hell of a battalion!

Called itself the 603rd Infantry Battalion. No bloody wonder! Maybe that was because there wasn't a 604th and because Oberkommando Wehrmacht had been scraping the bottom of the barrel when they'd spawned the 603rd. It looked like that, anyway! Most of the women and old men who'd lined the streets when the advance party had marched from the railway halt at the other end of the village had pointed derisively and laughed openly at such a raggle-taggle mix of schoolboys and pensioners.

'*Êtes-vous SS?*' they'd jeered. '*SS? Grossdeutschland Panzer Korps, peut-être? N'est-ce pas?*'

And when they howled at their own wit the Germans had taken it all on the chin and their elderly officers had marched at the head of their troops each with his eyes fixed unwaveringly to the front, shoulders erect in as near a military bearing as he could maintain. But the French had no doubt at all that this was a fifth, sixth or even a seventh-rate German formation. Everyone who had lined the streets that day knew it and their morale had blossomed in the knowledge.

Even so, there was another side to the coin. The village was situated well within the perimeter of Vichy France – the Unoccupied Zone. Then why were there to be German combat troops in Talmont-les-deux-Ponts? Was it significant that the Allies had recently forced landings along the Baie de la Seine in Normandy?

Vague and inconclusive explanations had been given to the mayor and his councillors by the German Commanding Officer, Oberstleutnant Lothar Overath, who had gone out of his way to settle his troops in amicably with the French villagers. He'd insisted there were no problems in Talmont, but believed that extra precuations were being taken in St Etienne and Lyon. There, heavily-armed bands of Resistance fighters were reported to be sabotaging main roads and railways, in an attempt to stem the flow of armour and supplies from the German panzer divisions in the south of France to the Normandy battlefronts. The 603rd Infantry Battalion was in reserve. It had been mustered in Westphalia only three months ago. The soldiers had no battle experience and had little field training. It was unlikely they'd ever be called upon to help in Normandy. They'd probably remain here in Talmont until the war was over – he'd shrugged – one way or the other!

And the mayor, René Dubois, had chuckled when he'd passed on these observations to the Regional Action Committee of the Franc Tireurs et Partisans. He'd explained that Overath must be sixty-years-old if he was a day and that he, Dubois, had got the idea that so far as the oberstleutnant was concerned, the war couldn't end too soon.

All very well and cosy, Armand Guerineau had answered. But that didn't alter the fact that the bastards were Boches and that they'd no right to come barging into Talmont-les-deux-Ponts. And what was more, by Christ, they wouldn't have dared to if they hadn't been carrying machine guns and flame throwers!

These were Boches bastards first – *sales Boches* – schoolkids and old age pensioners second! Let nobody in Talmont ever forget that! If the oberstleutnant believed he'd bought himself an easy ride with his sad, weak smile and a hint of collaboration, then he was in for a hell of a shock!

Thus the first two of his soldiers died on the bridge over the Loze river on the sixth night of their occupation of the village. They crumpled silently on to the *pavé*, the older man sprawling across the thin, undernourished form of the schoolboy. That was how it had to be!

Minutes passed before Guerineau and Simon emerged from the shadows of Pouroux's *boulangerie*, moving silently into the middle of the road where they could look up the slope of the bridge to where the German bodies lay.

They paused again, hesitant, frowning. Seconds passed. Then, when Guerineau motioned irritably, they turned round to hurry from the bridge and along a hundred metres of road to the Galberan barn, where they found the main doors had been opened to the road and that shadowy forms of men crouched in the inner darkness. They were wearing dark clothing, faces blackened, their hands clutching ·45-inch Thompson submachine guns which the United States Army Air Force had dropped them only a few days earlier. About their necks hung canvas holdalls heavy with primed grenades. Laced to their belts were new commando knives which the men had honed to razor keenness on the leather uppers of their boots as they'd whiled away the past couple of hours.

Simon grinned to himself as they parted to let him through. Kill-a-Boche-a-day! It could be that after tonight they were going to have a few days in hand!

Two hundred and fifty metres almost due west was a second bridge which also spanned the Loze river. But this was much smaller and narrower than that at the widening loop to the west and, for decades, had been limited to the passage of pedestrians, their hand-carts and cycles. Way back, six hundred years ago, it had been built for mules, ponies and dog-carts, and today even in a village as small as Talmont-les-deux-Ponts there wasn't an automobile narrow enough to squeeze between its stone parapets. Beneath it flowed the Loze, as peaceful and reassuring as ever to all who passed that way, many of them pausing to peer down into its slow-moving green depths and toss dry crusts to a colony of ducks which populated the banks on the downstream side.

That night, leaning against the parapet almost on the apex of the bridge, stood the lone figure of Siegfried Hornig. His rifle was propped up beside him and his thumbs thrust down the inside of his leather equipment belt – one each side of the *"Gott Mit Uns"* buckle – his thoughts many hundreds of miles away.

The balm of the summer's night with the half-moon riding high in a velvet sky and just tipping the tall pines on the distant horizon reminded him more than a little of home. His mind's eye was focused sharply on the cottage he'd shared with his wife, Irma, and his two young sons, Karl and Gunter, three kilometres from Meersburg/Bodensee, where for the past fifteen years he'd taught at the local village school.

He was staring into the sky above this French village he'd never heard of until a week ago and asking himself for the thousandth time why the Wehrmacht had suddenly decided to root him out of civilian niche. Maybe because there were no boys left in Germany to teach any more, he reflected wryly.
Maybe because . . . a rising cry strangled itself in his throat as Georges Chiarisoli's commando knife bit through his jugular vein and severed his windpipe, with all the man's pent-up hate concentrated in that single savage thrust.

Blood torrented over the German's M-44 field blouse with its economy-pattern insignia and triangular national emblem, the Hoheitsabzeichen looking pathetically new. Chiarisoli balanced himself precariously on the narrow stone ledge on the river-side of the parapet and lowered the body silently to the *pavé*.

He raised the thumb of his right hand as he picked his way back along the stone ledge to the riverbank, where the rest of the Maquis detachment was deployed amongst the darkened houses some fifty metres west of the bridge.

Marius Combin stepped out of the shadows to clasp his arm firmly.

'*Bon, Georges! Bon!*'

And as he whispered the words, so young Jean Martineau joined them and Combin nodded at once to the boy's unspoken question. Martineau put two fingers of his right hand into his mouth and, as he blew, so there rose the hunting cry of a barn owl above the silent village and the gurgling Loze river.

The three men waited, anxious now, for the shots from the east bridge had been Chiarisoli's signal to go forward and kill the German sentry here.

But, seconds later, came the all clear. To-woo! To-woo! Sharp and distinct. The Resistance fighters grouped around the buildings grinned at each other in nervous relief, the British-issue ·303-inch Lee Enfield rifles and the US-issue ·45-inch tommy-guns held lightly in their hands, rounds in the chambers, safety catches forward.

At the rear of the group an elderly man carried a captured German MG-42 machine gun. A full ammunition belt was already clipped into the breech and the three boys who stood beside him had more loaded belts slung about their necks. It was apparent that these men had had some experience with the rapid-firing Spandau, and having once run out of ammunition in a tight spot they were making damned sure it didn't happen a second time.

'Let's go!'

This was Marius Combin putting urgency into the command. 'Keep to your sections and when the shooting starts don't forget to move to the left of the *mairie*. We don't want to be knocking off each other, for Christ's sake!'

They moved off as an operational infantry formation with each successive section of eight men on alternate sides of the road. Their fingers were on their triggers, eyes roaming over the upper storeys of the houses and shops as they approached the centre of the village and the Place Gondin where the *mairie*

9

stood. They knew they were being watched because wives and parents had been warned of what was to happen that night. Better that the women and children should keep out of sight when the bullets began to fly. Even so, their anxiety wouldn't let them sleep – that was for sure! So, as the men moved silently along the dark streets they could occasionally glimpse the curtains of those upstairs rooms stir as they passed by.

To their right was the three-metre-wide riverside walk with the tall elms separating it from the paved road at one side and with century-old iron railings topping the bank at the other. To most of the men it was heartening to move freely about the town again after a week of the Boche curfew – soon again to lean against those iron railings at midnight with a glass of red wine in one hand and a smouldering Gauloise in the other!

At the junction with the riverside walk and the Rue Gondin the two Maquis detachments converged. Guerineau acknowledged Combin with a lift of a hand and the latter grinned amiably as he looked back at his own men. This was good liaison! Together, they'd a force of upwards of eighty well-armed and reliable troops. More than enough to handle two companies of inferior Boche infantry, even if there were three hundred of the bastards. Tonight they'd learn that rural France was no haven from the Allied bombing of their Fatherland!

They spread out along the Rue Gondin up to within a few metres of the junction at which it merged into the Place Gondin. This was a large square, even for a French village, with a wide perimeter road which completely encircled both the *mairie* and the Auberge de la Bobotte, clustered close together on an irregular circle of grass and oil-stained concrete.

Guerineau and Combin moved towards the square together, keeping to the shadows. Now they could see that both buildings, requisitioned and occupied by the 603rd Infantry Battalion Headquarters and two companies of infantry, were ablaze with lights. They looked at each other and grinned. Even these amateurs weren't stupid enough to turn down the lights in an occupied French town!

The foyer of the hotel which, until its recent occupation, had been a popular port of call for local agricultural workers and visiting farmers, had been converted into a makeshift guard-room. There was an MG-42 machine gun, tripod-mounted, by

10

the open double doors and the shining black coal-scuttle helmets of the guards could be glimpsed through the windows. In the forecourt at the top of three wide, stone steps were two sentry boxes and in front of each stood a soldier in full battle equipment, with a G-41 (M) 7·92mm rifle with fixed bayonet slung over his shoulder. This was an operational guard and it followed that there would be others positioned at strategic points around the buildings.

The men with the anti-tank weapons took up position on the pavement. Guerineau and Combin watched them settle themselves into firing positions down at the kerbside, lift the cumbersome weapons to their shoulders and take a trial aim. When they had raised their hands in confirmation that they were on target Guerineau yelled '*Fire!*' and before the cry had left his lips two hollow-charge bombs had slammed into the wall of the German guardroom and exploded in a single blinding flash.

To the Maquis there came immediate blurred impressions of the two German sentries disintegrating before their eyes in a sudden explosion of bone, sinew and blood. Lumps of their torn flesh hurtled across the street to splash into the wall against which the main force was grouped.

Combin lifted a hand to dash a gobbet of blood pulp from his hair. By this time the six other men of the leading section were lobbing phosphorous bombs into the mounting flames of the guardroom and through the shattered windows of the second storey.

Somewhere inside, alarm bells began to ring. There followed hoarse, guttural cries in German verging on panic; and, as the first soldiers leapt from the burning building into the street, so the Maquis opened up with machine guns, MP-40 Schmeiser machine pistols and rifles. They fired from the hip whilst moving into better cover along the north side of the square, whilst those at the rear of the column passed behind them to enfilade the east and west sides with sufficient overlap to neutralise any attempt at a German withdrawal.

The chatter of Maquis small-arms fire was building up to a crescendo with little retaliation from the German infantry. Long tongues of flame interlaced with curling black smoke began to lick into the second and third storeys of both buildings and frantic, naked figures crowded these windows with their hands already raised in surrender.

Guerineau roared above the pandemonium, pointing.

11

'Let the bastards have it!'

But it was apparent to the Frenchmen that there would be no resistance from these high windows. The Germans were screaming now as the flames lapped their unprotected bodies. A few had already leapt to the ground, their shrieks rising above the noise of the gunfire as they plummeted to the cobbles with a velocity which shoved their thigh bones high into their bodies or cracked open their skulls like walnuts.

Guerineau and Combin knew by this time that their battle was won, for the Germans who had managed to escape and were still capable of movement were already surrendering, their young-old faces ashen and gaunt in the glare of the fires.

Guerineau clapped his friend on the shoulder. This was something the Boches hadn't expected in the Unoccupied Zone, wasn't it? *Sales Boches*! They hadn't expected death by burning. Not when their officers had gone out of their way to be friendly and understanding towards the villagers.

And, on their part, the Germans were aware that these were not soldiers' deaths they were dying. They were being systematically murdered only for hate. And that hate wasn't concentrated solely at them, but at the hundreds of thousands of other German soldiers who had pillaged France over the past years. Now it was they who were having to pay the price! The 603rd Infantry Battalion. To settle somebody else's account – and for what? The battle for France was already as good as lost.

The Maquis streamed their fire into the fleeing, pain-crazed German infantry, bowling them over like skittles as they ran forward, their arms raised and their mouths working in indecipherable pleas for mercy. But the Frenchmen's faces remained as hard and as uncompromising as those of the SS officers and Gestapo agents they had seen so many times before. Now, at long last, France had found her teeth and the weakest had to pay. What did it matter if these were seventeen-year-old schoolboys or forty-five-year-old grandfathers? They were all Germans, weren't they? And the only good Boche was a dead Boche!

German casualties were piling up in concentric circles around the burning buildings, charred timber from the upper window frames floating down on top of them and causing the wounded to intensify their screams as they attempted to crawl away from this new torture. All around, the dead sprawled with their uniforms ablaze, the warm appetising smell of roasting human flesh picked up by air currents which drifted towards the Maquis gunners.

It was as a secondary explosion suddenly billowed from the north side of the square that Jean Latour moved forward to the corner of the Rue Gondin, where Marius Combin was controlling his detachment of automatic weapons. He tapped Combin on the shoulder and when he turned, Latour grinned unconcernedly at him, pointing to the blaze.

'We'll have to move in, Marius!' he said. 'We agreed to let the Mairie and the Auberge go. Not the whole bloody village!'

Combin grimaced and shot a glance at Guerineau, who had seen Latour approach and guessed what the man had in mind. Latour played a key role in the Maquis plans of attack for he was the village fire chief – *chef des pompiers* – and as he'd just said to Combin, it would be self-defeating to let the whole village burn itself out.

'Cease fire!'

Guerineau reacted immediately and the machine gun, machine pistol and rifle fire chattered into a ragged silence which gave way to the crackle of the flames and the cries of the German infantry.

'Watch your fronts!' Guerineau shouted. 'But shoot only if you have to. Make way for the *pompiers*!'

And, as the ranks of Maquis parted, through the gap raced the voluntary fire fighters of Talmont-les-deux-Ponts, unreeling their hoses as they ran.

The Maquis watched anxiously, knowing just how vulnerable these brave men were, for their work only had to do with the survival of the village and nothing at all with the dead and wounded Germans. But by the time they had reached the corner of the Place Gondin their colleagues along the river-bank had started up their pumps and jets of water began to arc not at the burning buildings, but on to a row of cottages and the two cafe-bars which skirted the north side.

The Maquis gunners tightened their trigger fingers, aware there was a chance of a German counterattack, but none came. Then they reminded themselves that these were not SS men. Not even established Wehrmacht! These were young lads and old men of the 603rd Infantry Battalion who wouldn't have the guts, the dedication or the know-how to launch a frontal attack across twenty metres of *pavé* into the machine guns of seasoned Resistance fighters. As far as these Boches were concerned, it was all over. The bastards were either shrivelled to cinders or cowering in the cellars, praying to their German God that a miracle might spare the Master Race.

Well – one had! The fires could well be beyond control. The *pompiers* had had to take over!

'Come out with your hands up! Slowly and in single file! Move yourselves or we start to toss in grenades!' Guerineau moved recklessly into the middle of the road as he shouted. He was unarmed and he stood with his legs braced, head held back, his broad shoulders squared. 'If you've officers amongst you, then let 'em come out first!'

For about thirty seconds nothing happened and the Maquis stood poised clutching British Mills bombs, thumbs and forefingers gripping the firing-pin rings. They'd have liked nothing better than to have blasted into the wine cellars, but suddenly movement came from within the burning frame of the entrance to the Auberge de la Bobotte.

They saw a German officer standing there holding a short pole at the end of which a piece of white material had been tied. The man hesitated beneath the burning door frame, looking like a performing dog at a circus. Then he lunged forward to the top of the three steps where he stumbled over a number of bodies which lay there naked, their flesh rippling red in the heat from the fire and streaked black with falling charcoal. He managed to right himself and as he did so he lifted high the pole.

Behind him came a thin, bent figure, eyes roaming over the dead. He hesitated as though in two minds as to whether he should turn back into the burning hotel and lose himself amongst the flames. But he pulled back his thin shoulders in much the same way as the officer with the flag had done and halted on the top step, with more smouldering timber dropping in showers of sparks around him.

'I am Oberstleutnant Overath!' he called in a voice which indicated courage and reflected little of the man's physical frailty. 'If you are prepared to hold your fire I will bring out the remainder of my troops!'

Guerineau took a couple of steps forward.

'You must come alone, Colonel!'

Overath hesitated again, then he strode down the steps into the road and crossed to where Guerineau was standing. A

14

spontaneous ragged cheer arose from the Maquis to be taken up and echoed in the houses around the square where windows had been suddenly thrown open and were crowded with women and young children. The cheers intensified as the German battalion commander halted in front of Guerineau.

There was a sad smile on his face as he said quietly, 'You win today, my friend! But soon you will lose. And how you will lose! You must know as well as I that Oberkommando Wehrmacht will not tolerate an outrage such as this.' He shrugged helplessly. 'There are SS regiments in the region. The streets of your village will run red with French blood!'

But Guerineau shook his head.

'This is 1944, Colonel!' he replied sharply. 'The Allies have broken through from Caen. The American 3rd Army is already looping south. Your SS will have far more to worry about than what has happened in Talmont-les-deux-Ponts. That is why you're here! You and your 603rd Infantry Battalion. The best that Oberkommando can produce!' His voice hardened and dissolved the sneer in the last few words. 'So bring out your brave survivors, Colonel! And mark that at the first sign of resistance they will be shot! You understand that?'

Overath nodded gravely and lifted a hand to beckon to two officers who had come halfway across the road to join him. At his signal they turned around and hurried to the iron doors alongside the stone steps which led into the wine cellars beneath the Auberge. One of them shouted orders and there came the sound of heavy bolts being withdrawn, the wrench of ancient hinges, and the wary cries of the soldiers who had found shelter amongst the wine racks from the flames of the burning buildings and the bullets of the Maquis.

Seconds later a ragged line of German soldiers came up the steps into the road, many as naked as when they had panicked down the burning stairs to the cellars. Now they shambled forward under the taunting eyes of the French, their heads lowered in their shame and in a bitter anger towards the officers who had let this happen to them. The 603rd would never have been a frontline infantry battalion but, by God, they could have done better than this!

There were many more infantry in the cellars than the Maquis had anticipated and they watched them being herded into three untidy ranks which bulged around the heaps of bodies of their dead comrades. A feldwebel had taken

15

command and began numbering them off with some semblance of military discipline. Then he strode over to where Oberstleutnant Lothar Overath was standing with Guerineau and Combin.

He saluted smartly with eyes only for his commanding officer.

'Report a strength of one hundred and eighty-four, Herr Oberstleutnant!'

Overath eyed him gravely as he returned to the salute.

'Thank you, Feldwebel!' Then he turned back to Guerineau. 'How many prisoners do you have, *m'sieu*?'

Guerineau shrugged.

'Forty? Maybe fifty?'

He pointed over to the north side of the square where a section of his Maquis had herded a group of German infantrymen into a cul-de-sac between two tall buildings. 'We haven't checked, yet. But let us say fifty!' He swung an arm which took in the dead and wounded lying on the *pavé*. 'Then how many casualties, Herr Oberstleutnant? Together. Dead and wounded.'

Overath shrugged.

'Perhaps the same number as your estimate of prisoners. Perhaps fifty.'

'Good!' Guerineau came back at him harshly. 'You appreciate that you and they are all now prisoners of the Franc Tireurs et Partisans?'

'For the time being, perhaps!'

Guerineau laughed at that.

'For the time being? I see that you have still much to learn, Herr Oberstleutnant.'

'And I must remind you that you have wounded amongst your prisoners of war. They need medical treatment!'

Guerineau laughed again as he turned to glance at Combin.

'Are you serious, Herr Oberstleutnant?' he asked. 'Have you ever heard of the French Resistance making medical supplies available to the German occupying forces?'

Overath's face remained impassive.

'As you know, *m'sieu*,' he said quietly, 'I am not acquainted with the principles of the French Resistance. I have priorities only for my own troops. Many are badly injured. They must have medical supplies and hospital care! As an officer I was taught to treat a defeated enemy with compassion.'

16

'And that was in 1918?'

'Primarily.'

Guerineau shook his head resignedly.

'Then it is sad that you have not been brought up to date by your Nazi commanders. For in 1944 there is no place for such compassion. Here there are only live and dead Germans and the more there are of the latter the happier we shall be! But all right. My men will escort you and your wounded to the agricultural sheds alongside the schoolhouse beyond the square. But if any of them try to escape or your officers attempt to establish contact with either Oberkommando Wehrmacht or your reserve companies, then hostages will be taken and shot! I hope you will understand that, too, Herr Oberstleutnant!'

Overath straightened his narrow back and nodded curtly.

'I understand perfectly, m'sieu! And perhaps, now, I might be allowed to attempt to salvage what is left of my command.'

Above the hills to the east the first grey hint of dawn had begun to tinge the sky and a haze was rising from the meandering Loze river which promised another day of sunshine.

And with the break in the night clouds, the villagers of Talmont-les-deux-Ponts began to warily emerge from their homes and come towards the Place Gondin. Only those who had lived facing the *mairie* and the Auberge de la Bobotte had witnessed the night's drama whilst the others, secure in their homes, had listened to the frantic cries of wounded men, the rattle of machine guns and the roar of the flames which had tinged their curtains vermilion. For them there had been no means of knowing whether the tide of battle was flowing the way of the Franc Tireurs et Partisans or the occupying German infantry.

By daylight the Place Gondin was crowded with people who wandered about unrestrained by the Maquis who still manned tactical and strategic vantage points. The German prisoners had been marched away, taking with them the dead and wounded. The scrape of their shovels in the stony earth beyond the schoolhouse could already be heard, as they dug a mass grave into which they would lay the charred, unidentified bodies of those of their comrades who had perished in the flames of the *mairie* and the Auberge de la Bobotte.

Yet, despite the Maquis' overwhelming victory, there were mixed feelings amongst the villagers who looked over the debris of the Place Gondin with dubious expressions. Over the past score of years and more there had been repeated demands made upon the village council to have the decrepit *mairie* and equally tumbledown *auberge* cleared away from the village centre. These demands had been forcibly resisted on the grounds that a major part of Talmont's heritage lay in the *mairie*, though no such claim could be made in respect of the hotel. In consequence, both had been allowed to crumble into dust in their own good time and the prospect of a tree-bordered open square which had been the dream of most villagers for as long as they could remember had never materialised.

Now, the Franc Tireurs et Partisans had, by their actions, forced the issue. All that still remained to be done was to cart away the heaps of broken masonry and charred timber and there, before them, would be the open square they had wanted for so long!

The four Leclerc brothers with their tractors would scrounge enough black market petrol to do most of the donkey work and there would be sufficient willing bodies amongst the young men and women of the village to provide the muscle. They'd straighten out the pavement, too; and then, when the war was finally won, they'd build themselves a new *mairie* in the open ground beyond the 'Quatorze' war memorial.

Besides, they'd knocked all hell out of the Boches! Maybe from now on they wouldn't be so impetuous in dropping off second-line infantry battalions. This could be a lesson for the whole of France to pursue – both Zones!

But the big question lay on the other side of the coin. How were the Germans likely to react? No one knew, for this was the Unoccupied Zone and, so far, there had been no parallel!

At the Château d'Aubigny, nine kilometres north of Talmont-les-deux-Ponts, Major Karl-Heinz Emmerich, Second-in-Command of the 603rd Infantry Battalion, was standing in full battle gear before the two reserve companies which were paraded by platoons across the circular forecourt of the château.

For Major Emmerich the night had been tense and fraught with speculation. Now, as he glanced up at the brightening sky above the majestic redstone turrets of the château, he felt no easier about the situation.

He hurriedly crossed the fifty metres to his command

18

schutzpanzerwagen and climbed aboard. They would use these half-tracks to swan across country when they got within striking distance of Talmont-les-deux-Ponts. It was a strategy the Maquis were unlikely to anticipate and would enable them to drive-in attacks from a number of directions simultaneously.

All the same, there was a dead weight lodged deep in Emmerich's stomach. Apart from the recent bombing raids on Dresden, he had witnessed no military action since the closing months of the 1914—18 war. This fact, coupled with the knowledge that not a man in the two companies under his command had yet fired a shot in anger, did nothing to boost the likelihood of a quick and easy victory in the battle which lay ahead.

Yet, he stood tall in the forward position of the schutzpanzerwagen with the MG-42 machine gunner at his side. His was an arrogant, military figure, and one which could put heart into the men who were to follow him against guerilla fighters who were probably better equipped than they were.

What happened next was in the lap of the gods, Emmerich told himself. His plan had been agreed upon, officers and NCOs briefed, objectives defined and battle-phases meticulously calculated. He gave the order to move off to the officer commanding the 3rd Company in crisp tones. But, even at a good forced-march pace with fit healthy troops, the nine kilometres to Talmont-les-deux-Ponts would take well over an hour. With the kind of soldiers he'd got under his command it could take twice that time!

Not only that, the damned Maquis would be able to observe their approach all the bloody way!

Emmerich's big problem had been the lack of any kind of contact between himself and his commanding officer, Oberst-leutnant Lothar Overath, or, in fact, with anybody else in the Talmont-les-deux-Ponts force. What had happened in that village during the night was anybody's guess!

He had been awakened in his great four-poster bed a little after two am by the duty officer, who had shaken him diffidently and reported that sounds of small-arms fire had been heard in the occupied village and that buildings also appeared to be on fire there.

Emmerich had climbed irritably from his bed and gone over to the high oriel windows, to gaze across the distance to where a red glow in the sky silhouetted the tall pines across the park.

Yes! Certainly there was fire! And his ears told him there was also some automatic small-arms fire. Could be machine gun or machine pistol. At that distance it wasn't possible to isolate the distinctive prrt-prrt-prrt of the MG-42 Spandau. Even so, something was evidently wrong in the village.

But Emmerich showed no signs of panic or even of urgency. He believed that with whatever had developed in Talmont-les-deux-Ponts Overath's two companies were more than able to cope. Now he could go back to his bed and leave his CO to look after his own responsibilities.

But he didn't ...

Instead, he led the duty officer up the magnificent seventeeth-century staircase to the third floor, where the battalion's Signal HQ had been established and where two private soldiers were playing chess in front of a dead field R/T set.

They sprang to attention as the two officers entered the room, as diffident towards the major's striped dressing robe as they would have been to his full ceremonial dress uniform.

Emmerich waved them back into their chairs impatiently.

'Get me Oberstleutnant Overath!'

'Sir!'

The signallers acknowledged the order simultaneously and clamped on earphones, whilst one of them began spinning the dials of the R/T set. When he had established the frequency he called:

'Hello, Sunray One! This is Sunray Two! Are you receiving me? Over!'

The signaller lifted his head with the suggestion of a smile about his lips as he caught the duty officer's eye. But, seconds later, this was replaced by a frown as he turned back to his dials, now edging them delicately with thumb and forefinger.

He called again: 'Hello, Sunray One! This is Sunray Two! Are you receiving me? Over!'

Emmerich began to demonstrate his impatience and swung round to his duty officer.

'What the hell's happening, Vogel?'

The leutnant lifted an anxious face from the signaller and shook his head. Obviously, the man wasn't getting through. Emmerich glared maliciously at him and then turned unexpectedly on his heels and strode from the room, turning at the door to shout over his shoulder:

'You stay here, Vogel, and let me know the instant contact has been established!'

'Very good, Herr Major!'

Emmerich hurried down one flight of stairs to the room which had been appointed as orderly room to administer the two companies of his reserve command. There he dropped heavily into the chair behind his desk, pounding the embossed leather top with a balled fist. Damn these bloody signallers! Why was it that whenever they were needed their bloody sets would never function?

He raised his eyes to stare through the windows as he had on the floor below, contemplating why Overath hadn't troubled to keep him informed. But the more he pondered, the more he convinced himself that whatever was happening in the village couldn't be all that important. Maybe it was no more than some ordinary village fire. A barn blaze? But, if that was so, then how did it account for the small-arms fire? His irritability increased at his own inability to decide on a logical reason.

Then, a couple of minutes later, Leutnant Hans Vogel joined him with his face as blank as it had been in the Signals HQ.

'There's no reply from the CO, sir!' he announced. 'They've simply got no one manning the R/T. We've checked out circuits and we've checked transmission with our outposts. Everything's working at this end! It's just that Battalion Headquarters aren't acknowledging.'

He stopped speaking as likely explanations parallel to Emmerich's entered his mind . . . it could be nothing! Nothing at all. No more than a house or a farm fire . . . but . . .

'We could send a DR, sir?'

Emmerich looked at the young officer and nodded. This was the only option left open to them – short of detailing a full-scale fighting patrol and then looking like bloody idiots for doing so!

'All right!' he agreed. 'Detail a motorcycle combination, and make damned sure they maintain R/T contact with this HQ and that the signallers upstairs don't bloody-well lose it!'

So it was that half an hour later, Major Karl-Heinz Emmerich learnt of the defeat and humiliation of the Battalion Headquarters and two rifle companies of the 603rd Infantry Battalion. The two-man motorcycle combination crew reported as much in that same orderly room with faces pallid and their limbs unsteady at what they had witnessed. Initially, their statements lacked coherence, but Emmerich had the

21

patience to accept that these were unblooded troops who, until minutes ago, had never seen a German soldier die in battle.

Subsequently, in their own time, they went on to describe how they had parked their vehicle in a copse about a kilometre short of the village perimeter. There, they had unclipped the Spandau from its sidecar mounting and picked their way along the hedgerows towards the dark line of buildings which were silhouetted against the red sky.

They had listened to the cries of German wounded. The soldiers shrieking in their agony! Pleading for a quick bullet and death! 'They were being burned alive, Herr Major!'

'Who was burning them alive?'

'The French! French civilians! They were machine-gunning our men as they tried to get clear of the fires. There were French women who laughed as they saw them drop from the hotel windows into the flames! The whole square was on fire, sir!'

'Are you telling me you saw this happen? Saw it yourselves?'

The machine gunner pointed to the driver. 'It was Maier who went forward. I covered. Maier saw it happen, sir!'

Emmerich stared hard at the boy.

'We had two companies in Talmont, Maier. All right! So some of our troops were in action with French civilians. Then what were the rest of them doing?'

Maier shook his head.

'There were no other soldiers, Herr Major! There were only the dead and burning. The rest were prisoners.'

'Prisoners? Prisoners? How many for God's sake?'

'Couldn't say, sir. Columns of 'em! Maybe a hundred and fifty! Two hundred! I couldn't be sure . . .'

So, now, with the first hint of dawn, the two reserve companies of the 603rd Infantry Battalion were formed up in the forecourt of the Château d'Aubigny, preparing to move into battle.

They had no infantry guns other than the 2mm cannons mounted on each of the three schutzpanzerwagen half-tracks. Neither did they have infantry transporters. They had no alternative but to march the distance to the village, before they could make an assessment of the tactical possibilities and confirm their pre-arranged plan of attack.

At best, they would have to rely upon their standard

infantry arms – rifles and automatic weapons, a couple of 5cm Granatwerfer 36 mortars and a limited supply of stick grenades which had already been distributed amongst the point sections.

This was going to be a dicey situation, for the Maquis would observe every move of their advance and, besides, there was no telling their strength or the fire-power of their weapons!

Emmerich shook his head as his schutzpanzerwagen jerked on its tracks to move into position behind the leading platoon.

Christ! If ever there was a way to blunder blindly into an ambush, then this must surely be it!

That much he knew, but he'd rather have charged headfirst into a concentrated cone of fire from a Maquis machine gun than have reported such a bizarre situation to either Oberkommando Wehrmacht, St Etienne, or to the 32nd Panzer Division, Waffen SS Uber Alles which he knew had recently moved into the region.

Apart from the basic fact that Talmont-les-deux-Ponts was Wehrmacht occupied, Yves Mercier, Commander-in-Chief of the Franc Tireurs et Partisans, Region Monique, had had three other reasons for selecting the village as an action centre for an all out Maquis-inspired offensive within the Unoccupied Zone.

Firstly, the village was reasonably isolated. Apart from the neighbouring farming hamlet of Villeneuf-sur-Loze, some six kilometres distant and boasting a total population of under fifty, there was no other town or village within a twenty kilometre radius.

Secondly, Talmont was situated in an ideal natural defensive location; not only against infantry assault, but also against medium tanks and half-tracked fighting vehicles. The Loze river which wound its way back and forth across the flat agricultural landscape was a perfect tank trap, with steep banks up to five or six metres deep in places and bordered by mature willows and alders substantial enough to screen anti-tank weapons. The Loze was also deep enough to engulf any infantrymen wearing assault equipment unwise enough to attempt to swim its deceptive width. Without doubt, the Loze was one hundred per cent French orientated and worth a hundred fighting men.

Thirdly, the terrain around the village was criss-crossed

with high and often impenetrable bocage hedges, most of which offered ideal sitings for defensive machine guns. A good gunner with an able Number 2 could turn defence into attack by doing little more than changing his position as and when the course of the battle dictated. The same applied to anti-tank weapons. A determined man handling a PIAT, a panzerfaust, or an American bazooka, could knock out half-a-dozen panzers without being called upon to reveal his position. In most places the Boches' armour would be restricted to the roads and lanes, anyway.

Both Armand Guerineau and Marius Combin, who had accepted personal responsibility for the success of the operation, shared Mercier's conviction that there could have been no more suitable location than Talmont-les-deux-Ponts. And, as an added bonus, there was also the pyschological fact that most of the villagers wanted the centre of their village demolished to make room for improvements. In consequence, the final gilt on the gingerbread had been that the Germans had by chance selected these very two buildings to house half their battalion strength!

What, for Christ's sake, could have been a better incentive to success?

So it was that on the morning following the humiliating defeat of the German 603rd Infantry Battalion, as the first grey shafts of dawn braced the distant horizon, Armand Guerineau pushed out his first reconnaissance patrols. These he deployed tactically, regardless of the fact that the two remaining support companies of the 603rd Infantry Battalion were known to be located at the Château d'Aubigny nine kilometres to the north. During the past three years in the rough and tumble of the Pas de Calais region, Guerineau had learnt the hard way the value of systematic all-round defence. Even so, his main strike force still remained concentrated east of the village, and it was through this concentration that the patrols marched to take up prepared positions which had been meticulously sited and planned a week earlier.

There were mortar pits in which the location of the heavy base plates had been etched into the turf, and there were narrow strips of wood stuck into the earth along the rims of the weapon pits on which pre-calculated ranges had been marked. There were also ditches cut into the ground at the rear of the emplacements to house the steel boxes of high explosive mortar bombs. Similarly, there were also machine gun and rifle positions in which ranges had also been marked and the surrounding undergrowth cleared to widen the gunners' field of fire. Further forward were slit-trenches to house volunteer tank-destroyers, perfectly sited at those places where panzers, coming unexpectedly under fire, were likely to sheer off the road across country.

All in all, this was a fine defensive complex, expertly planned and executed and one which Guerineau and his field commanders knew was sound enough to halt not only the 603rd Infantry Battalion, but also the Waffen SS itself!

Admittedly, in time the SS would eventually and systematically carve themselves a path through even such a labyrinth of defensive earthworks, but they wouldn't find it easy and they wouldn't make it without more casualties than they could afford in a single confrontation with guerillas.

Here, the Maquis planned to make a name for themselves and Talmont-les-deux-Ponts was a village which would be remembered by Oberkommando Wehrmacht for a long time to come! The only thing they lacked was direct artillery support, but the Boches didn't have much of that either. And, what was more, they'd be wary of using what they had when shelling a village in which their own wounded were laid out on stretchers across the village square.

Guerineau watched his patrols leave the Place Gondin with a confident wave of his hand. Good men all of 'em! Bloody true men of France! They couldn't lose!

It was about half an hour later that preliminary R/T reports began to come through to Guerineau. As they crackled through earphones rich with static he smiled confidently at his lieutenant, Marius Combin.

'The Boches are stuck!' he told him. 'Corsin reports that their point platoons have reached the intersection with Jacques' farm. The stupid buggers have come too far! See our map, reference 847385. They can't turn their vehicles in those lanes.'

Combin grinned, too.

'So we let them come close. What armour have they got?'

'Armour? Very little! So far we've spotted three schutzpanzerwagens mounting 2mm cannons and that seems to be the lot. We might even take 'em instead of just brewing 'em up. What do you say?'

Behind his two leading platoons of infantry, Major Karl-Heinz Emmerich halted his command schutzpanzerwagen and climbed down heavily over the track guard to stand in the centre of the narrow lane. There he remained for some minutes watching the infantry sections, heavily-laden in full battle gear, move past him at either side.

The surrounding terrain was as flat as a billiard table, with parallel lines of tall trees marking the winding flow of the Loze river. Directly ahead were the clustered sandstone buildings of Talmont-les-deux-Ponts, standing out warmly orange in the brightening dawn.

The village appeared calm and relaxed, just as it would on any work-day morning. There came the intermittent crowing of roosters, the lowing of distant cattle, and even though a tang of charred timber hung in the air there were no signs of smoke. Nothing other than a thin grey mist which was already rising from the meadows under the warming sun.

Despite the reports of his early morning motorcycle patrol, Major Emmerich began to wonder if his fears had been no more than morbid speculation brought on by the tensions of living an isolated existence and encircled by hate. Judging by what he could make out from his position two kilometres east of the village, this was just one more summer's day. More than likely, Oberstleutnant Overath had been quick to put an end to the trouble which had sprung up amongst a rabble of excited Frenchmen reacting to a village fire.

He scowled as another infantry section pushed its way between himself and the bulk of the parked schutz-panzerwagen. It struck him how old some of these conscripted soldiers were, and he asked himself what kind of a fight they'd put up against a fanatical band of Resistance fighters whose one ambition was to settle in five minutes their scores of five years of German dominance.

He glanced up at his signaller, sitting high in the half-track with his earphones clamped over his bare head and the long radio antenna weaving under the vibration from the engine.

'Anything coming through?'

He guessed this was a pointless question even as he spoke the words, but he had to make a final check before committing his force.

The signaller shook his head. 'No contact, Herr Major!'

'Come down now. We go forward on foot from here.' Then

26

to the schutzpanzerwagen commander, a grizzled feldwebel wearing long-service stripes on his sleeve, he called; 'Join the other two! God knows what you can do in this kind of country, but stand by to use your cannons on call!'

As a personal escort, Emmerich peeled off a section of five riflemen and an MG-42 machine gun crew of three, diverting their line of advance directly across country towards the village.

A half-kilometre further on, they came upon the east bank of the Loze river where he halted the section and squatted in the long grass at a point where there was sufficient open ground to use his binoculars. There he remained, waiting for the rest of the force to take up their pre-determined positions along a kilometre stretch of that same riverbank.

Still, nothing appeared to be happening ahead, and the only sound reaching his ears was the movement of his own troops through the long grass. If the Maquis were about, then they must be dug in and waiting, he told himself. And, if so, then clearly they didn't intend to make the first move. Their plan would be primarily defensive – and whose wouldn't be in this kind of country? The French were going to sweat it out and take up the battle in their own good time!

He turned to his signaller.

'Call company commanders to an 'O' Group!' he ordered him tersely. And when Hauptmann Konrad Horchem and Hauptmann Bruno Michelfeld squirmed into cover at his side he wasted no time in voicing his problem.

'We've got to break this damned deadlock!' He thumped the ground in front of him with a clenched fist, anger at his own impotence lifting his tone. 'We'll put in a probing attack and see what it rouses! Over there, to the right, where the copse screens that side of the village. Horchem! Take two platoons of Number 4 Company. Quickly as you can!' He scowled myopically at the dial of his wristwatch shaded by the trees. 'Twenty minutes?' He looked up again at the hauptmann with the question still in his eyes. 'Can you attack in twenty minutes?'

Horchem, a young officer who had spent the past year as an instructor at an infantry battle school in Mainz, looked doubtful.

'There's the river, Herr Major!' He pointed into the depths of the Loze which in that light looked grim and foreboding.

27

'There are no crossing points. We'll have to rig up rope bridges ...'

'What the hell, Horchem! You're not planning a bloody assault course now! I'm asking you if you can get a couple of platoons over there within twenty minutes?'

Horchem still hesitated, but then he thrust back his head and replied, 'Very well, Herr Major! Twenty minutes!' He glanced at his watch. 'At five-ten, precisely, we'll move into the attack.'

Emmerich turned to Michelfeld.

'You will liaise with Horchem and provide covering fire. When Number 4 Company has established positions close to the village, you will go forward under their cover. I shall call a second 'O' Group as and when circumstances dictate. All right! No questions! Get on with your preparations!'

Armand Guerineau had established a good three-quarters of his troops east of the village. Radio reports which had come in non-stop from forward patrols and OPs had indicated that the commander of the two German reserve companies had decided upon a frontal attack on the village. The news pleased Guerineau and he warmed to the coming showdown, knowing that his main problem now no longer lay primarily with the Wehrmacht, but also in controlling the reaction from amongst the civilian population. Already there had been some scathing and anxious comments, mainly from the women who'd not anticipated a prolongation of the night's conflict.

What had happened in Talmont-les-deux-Ponts had been little short of total war and whilst, at the time, they'd cheered themselves hoarse at the Franc Tireurs et Partisans' victory, they were becoming increasingly worried about the possibility of vicious reprisals from other German sources – for instance, the Gestapo and the Waffen SS! Futhermore, in such an eventuality they would be alone, for the Maquis would not commit themselves to a prolonged battle. They hadn't the staying power or the arms for that and, as ever, their plan would be to drive home their offensive and then make a rapid withdrawal with as few casualties as possible. Subsequently, they would repeat their programme at some other carefully pre-selected location with an equal likelihood of success.

Unfortunately, this meant that those who had to remain behind would have to brave the German wrath, and the ironic

28

thing about that was that they were in no way equipped to cope, either mentally or physically.

So that morning, Guerineau and Combin had sensed the cooling attitude towards the Maquis which experience had warned them to expect.

Of course, there would be Boches reprisals. There always were! And they were usually made against helpless French civilians, unarmed and vulnerable.

But, on the other hand, the Unoccupied Zone had had a doddle of a war compared with their compatriots in the north. So now they couldn't grumble too much when they'd been called upon to make a few sacrifices of their own!

The role of the Franc Tireurs et Partisans wasn't to ease the lot of French civilians. It was to kill Boches! To kill the bastards! Every single one that polluted the French countryside with his presence. Whether they were Wehrmacht, Waffen SS, or Gestapo was immaterial so long as enough of them died.

At five-ten, in line with Emmerich's battle plan, the forward platoons of Number 4 Company began to mount the west back of the Loze river at a point one and a half kilometres east-north-east of the village.

They had experienced problems crossing the river, as Horchem had anticipated they would. Men, unskilled in fieldcraft, had floundered in the deep water and there had been scenes close to panic as the combined weight of equipment and weapons had dragged them into the green depths. There was also a clammy chill about the water they hadn't expected and the new danger of death by drowning had momentarily taken precedence over the battle yet to be fought.

Now they lined the western bank, cowering amongst the undergrowth and tall grasses, their machine guns and platoon mortars sited in what natural folds in the ground they could find. They were also being observed and they knew it.

Hauptmann Konrad Horchem scoured the distant buildings of the village and the hedgerows between through binoculars, but not a blade of grass or a stone stirred. It was already a couple of minutes past his 'H' Hour. Emmerich would be beefing on the R/T if he didn't move now. Michelfeld's Number 3 Company was standing by to give them covering fire across the open ground. He hoped to hell they were! But, for Christ's sake, unless they were quick in spotting the muzzle

29

flashes of the French automatic weapons, then what did they plan to shoot at? It was a diccy venture! Even for seasoned troops. Too bloody dicey for comfort!

He pushed himself up into a sitting position, shoving the binoculars back into their case and taking the 9mm Walther P38 automatic from the holster at his belt.

'Number One Platoon!'

His voice rang strident through the morning air, the first sound to break the stillness since the rooster had ceased its crowing. He turned to the line of riflemen crouched at his right hand, conscious of their anxious and uncertain faces. These men weren't bloody fools! They were probably a damned sight brighter than most he'd come across in the SS. They'd had more time to be! They knew well enough what they were up against. If two infantry companies could seemingly disappear without trace in the middle of the night, then they were in for no walk-over themselves!

'Number One Platoon!' It would be crazy to risk his entire force in one assault, even if Michelfcld was covering. They'd take the first objective in two bounds. A two-phase operation . . . 'First bound will be the hedgerow three hundred metres directly ahead. Number Two Platoon keep your eyes skinned and be prepared to give supporting fire. One Platoon! Prepare to move! Move . . . now!'

And as he shouted the order so he, too, leapt to his feet ahead of the wavering line of thirty-odd infantrymen. He looked to his flanks as he increased his pace to a steady jog across the open meadow, thinking how bloody vulnerable they were in this inept attempt at a frontal assault.

But nothing happened . . .

They crossed their point of no-return, breathing silent prayers that the Maquis had pulled out of the village and called off their private war.

Please God!

Now they had only sixty or seventy metres still to go to their initial bound. Sixty metres and they'd be down in cover again, supporting Number Two Platoon who'd double over this same distance to join them. Then they'd both be in position for a combined assault on the village. Maybe it was going to be easy. Maybe they'd been lucky. Maybe the French had already cleared off!

Less than fifty metres to go.

Then: di-di-di-dah . . . a British Bren gun calmly tapping out the Allied 'V' for Victory sign in morse!

Di-di-di-dah!

The men of Number One Platoon glanced at each other with paling faces, half-expecting to see some of their number falling. But the Bren was shooting high.

Intentionally?

Way back amongst the buildings of the village, Armand Guerineau smiled to himself as he watched the battle scene developing before him. Some light machine gunner was being smart and he wondered who it was. But the man wasn't being stupid, for the Maquis had all the time in the world to hurl this laboured attack back to where it had sprung from − into the Loze river!

Seconds later, as though inspired by the call to action of the Bren, the full fire-power of the Maquis forward defensive line opened up and, with it, Horchem's point platoon threw themselves to the ground − less than thirty metres from their first bound. But they knew they hadn't a chance in hell of making it and, as they desperately clawed themselves into the ground, so the heads began to fly off the poppies and cornflowers in front of them. At first they couldn't understand why. The flower heads just sprang into the air for no apparent reason. But when the Maquis machine guns lifted their range, the singing of the bullets about their ears gave them their answer.

Section leaders yelled to the men to look out for the muzzle flashes of the automatic weapons as Horchem had briefed them before the attack; but the few who had the courage to raise their heads above the grass could make out neither smoke nor flame against the greens of the bocage hedges.

Panic started amongst a rear section where a couple of men sprang to their feet to race back across the meadow towards the safety of the river, but the Maquis bullets caught up with them as they ran, chasing them like a fast-burning fuse and then picking them off their feet at their ease. The force of the cone of fire stripped the equipment from their backs and cut into their flesh with the fury of a crazed axe-man, so that blood and sinew spilled from them even as they ran.

At the river, Number Two Platoon of Number 4 Company, detailed for the second wave, froze where they lay. Half a kilometre to the left, Major Karl-Heinz Emmerich, already sensing that his offensive was going to be bogged down before it even got underway, snatched the hand microphone from his signaller.

'Get those men moving, Michelfeld, goddamn you! I can see it's getting tricky, but they can't hang on there. We'll put down more covering fire from here! Now see that they move!'

'Perhaps smoke, sir . . .?'

'Smoke? What the hell for? If we put down smoke then how are we to identify our targets? Now stand-by to follow up the first platoon, for Christ's sake!'

He thrust the microphone back at the signaller and swung round to where the schutzpanzerwagen's forward liaison officer was adjusting the dials of his own field radio, awaiting orders.

'You heard that, Schonfeld?' Emmerich said. 'Fire a couple of belts into that hedge immediately below the first row of buildings. We'll try and pick out specific targets as the assault progresses!'

And with that he sank back into the grass cresting the river-bank with binoculars again to his eyes, his expression both angry and anxious.

By this time, Number Two Platoon of Horchem's Number 4 Company were crouching on their haunches, clutching their weapons, poised on the balls of their feet and prepared to charge forward to that same hedge which was also to be their initial objective.

Seconds later, the three schutzpanzerwagens opened up with a tearing cannon bombardment laced with heavy machine gun fire which splattered against the walls of the houses and lopped off the branches of trees amongst the bocage hedge.

Michelfeld lifted an arm, half-standing so that the three sections of the platoon could see his signal. It was apparent to him they would not go alone and, whether Emmerich liked it or not, he really had no alternative other than to leave his own company and lead the platoon to link up with Horchem and his men pinned down in the open. Together they might stand a chance of making the first bound using a fire and movement drill. Then, as Number 3 Company joined the schutz-panzerwagens with a ragged fusillade, he yelled, 'Stand by to advance . . . Move!' He leapt to his feet as Horchem had done and, as with Horchem, these rifle sections were also slow off the mark, metres behind him. He swung round angrily on to the straggling lines as he increased his own pace.

'Double up! Double up!' he shouted. 'We've to clear this open ground! Run goddammit!'

The wavering line stiffened at his example, but the platoon had not covered more than twenty metres when there came the bump-bump-bump of heavy mortars firing from somewhere amongst the buildings ahead.

Michelfeld glanced up into the sky as he ran and it was easy enough to spot the bombs shooting upwards to their zenith. He knew that a good mortar man could keep as many as fifteen bombs in the air at any one time and pattern their dropping zone to keep pace with advancing infantry.

'Run! Run!' Again he yelled at the new threat and this time his cry was echoed by the section leaders. The Maquis machine guns had suddenly lost much of their terror. Death and mutilation were about to rain on them from the sky from which there was no cover.

The platoon reacted in near panic. They forgot all about being German soldiers and lowered their rifles from the port position to run blindly forward, stumbling in their battle gear over the clumps of grass and thistle.

But the Maquis, manning the British 3-inch heavy mortars had, from their meticulously sited positions, made allowances for such a reaction and decreased their ranges to compensate, so that the leading section charged headlong into the first salvo of bombs as they exploded.

Still with the main body at the Loze river, Emmerich saw this situation develop. To him it was like a nightmare in which he could see horrific things happening before his eyes and yet was unable to do anything about them. It was inevitable that high-explosive mortar bombs were going to burst amongst Number 2 Platoon whilst they were without cover.

He hunched his shoulders as though the bombs were ranged on him. And through their flat blasts he watched a second salvo, cleverly short-ranged, explode along the hedgerow which was to have been Number 4 Company's first bound. He dropped his head into his hands, accepting that their annihilation was a certainty.

Hauptmann Bruno Michelfeld was thinking what a pointless way this was to die, out here in some God forsaken French meadow, impotent against the inspired aggression of an organised body of French civilians and hundreds of kilometres from the real war. He was twenty-one-years-old and, by

Christ, he wasn't even leading his own company into this badly planned, badly executed, pointless assault! Back home he'd been a hero in the hamlet of Barrendorf in Westphalia — a Wehrmacht captain of infantry at twenty-one. And for what? To be blown to pieces in Talmont-les-deux-Ponts? That was a hell of a sick joke!

Still he ran with the inevitability of his death filling his mind. As long as he was running he was all right, he told himself. But the two hundred metres still to go to link up with Horchem's men might well have been two hundred kilometres. None of them stood a chance of making it. Not a bloody chance! Besides, the mortars had dropped their ranges again and the objective, itself, was bouncing under the bombardment.

A bomb exploded a few metres to his left and the force of the explosion caused him to swerve as he ran, almost blasting him off his feet. He shook himself, expecting pain and blood, but there was no sensation. But when he looked he saw that three of his men had fallen. The full force of the blast had scythed the shrapnel across their thighs. One soldier lay flat on his back with his legs severed and the man could see where his limbs lay on the ground a couple of metres away. He was still conscious. His eyes were staring from his head as he watched his legs jerk spasmodically and with each movement pump copious streams of blood from the shattered stumps. He dropped a hand to his thighs, his fingers groping into the jellied torn flesh there, and when he raised them to find them dripping with blood and sticky with sinew he began to scream.

A second man lay close by. The blast had lifted him from his feet and dropped him on to his head so that he huddled in a crouching position, paralysed, with his abdomen ripped open and his guts trailing back to the bomb burst where the shrapnel had first torn into his body. He, too, was conscious and from his crouched position looked on to an upside-down panorama, whilst the man with no legs screamed into his ears and another lay dead with a jagged lump of still-smoking shrapnel wedged into the side of his helmet as though it had been hammered there by a blacksmith.

Michelfeld absorbed these things into his brain as he continued to run, but they had little significance, merely part of a tableau from which he knew there could be no escape. Men were beginning to fall all around him and the mortar bombardment was giving way to more light machine gun fire. The

French bastards were machine-gunning the men they'd knocked over with their mortars. No prisoners! He recalled the warnings he'd received on his last home leave when he'd let it be known that he was expecting to be posted to the Unoccupied Zone . . . take care, the French Resistance take no prisoners!

Miraculously he was still running, rapidly closing the distance to the hedgerow directly ahead, where what remained of the mortar barrage was still pitching. It was bloody stupid to keep going in that direction, but what else could he do? He could put up his hands and trust to there being one Frenchman amongst the Maquis with a grain of compassion . . . what a hope!

A Bren gun picked him up, playing with him, the bullets keeping pace a metre and less in front of his aching legs, spurting up clods of turf and nipping off flower heads.

It was then that Hauptmann Bruno Michelfeld decided he'd had enough. Christ! He was a German officer! No homicidal French lunatic was going to make him run like this! He halted abruptly face crimson and streaming sweat as the bullets continued to rake ahead. Then he spread out his hands in a gesture which said: Here I am, do your damnedest! The French gunner smiled along the sights of his Bren gun and fired him a personal burst through the heart.

At the Loze river, Major Emmerich knew that this must be the end of his attempt to liberate his comrades in the village. It had been essential for Number 4 Company to make that first bound before the rest of the force could risk storming the village. Their only chance of success had hinged on that. Without it, there remained only failure; more German humiliation! His assault force had been obliterated – including a senior officer. The rest of the troops were still here on the wrong side of the river, as vulnerable as they'd ever been and half their initial strength. He began to sweat in a sudden fit of nervous exhaustion, gazing helplessly over the battlefield on which all the aggression and all the tactical advantages had been on one side.

The French small-arms fire died to a ragged silence. They, too, had accepted that the fighting was over and that they had only to mop up the inadequate and demoralised German survivors. It had been simple for them to notch up one more enemy infantry battalion amongst their scalps. This was one report which would make the radio waves sing all the way from the Communist Headquarters of the Franc Tireurs et Partisans to the Kremlin. More than likely to Josef Stalin, himself!

So what happened next?

He couldn't guess, but he knew now what he *should* have done. He should have been prepared to sacrifice his troop of schutzpanzerwagens in storming the east bridge over the Loze river into the village. He should have rushed them at the bridge with all the supporting small-arms fire his machine gunners and riflemen could put down. He should have mortared the bridge and charged his infantry behind the barrage in four or five waves, all of them screaming like dervishes with bayonets fixed. That's what he should have done! That had been the only way to confront the Maquis — man for man across the width of a village street!

But he'd been too anxious to avoid casualties. He'd tried the easy way out because he hadn't had the heart to throw schoolboys and middle-aged fathers against such French hate. Would an SS commander have hesitated under identical circumstances? He smiled sourly to himself. He'd have to pay the personal price of failure and that very soon! Perhaps with his life. In the meantime, he'd no alternative but to let the initiative remain with the Maquis.

It was Oberstleutnant Lothar Overath who made the next move.

He appeared alongside a private in battle gear who carried a pole to which a piece of white material had been tied.

Overath called through a loud-hailer.

'Major Emmerich! Is Major Emmerich over there?'

Emmerich got stiffly to his feet and strode from the trees to an open space where he could be seen.

'Sir!'

'Major!' The weariness in Overath's voice was apparent even above the resonance of the loud-hailer. 'I am informed that the French Maquis are to pull out within half an hour. Their commander informs me that providing you call off your offensive against the village during that period, he will order an immediate cease-fire. Understood?'

Emmerich lifted his eyes heavenwards, not sure that such salvation was for himself or for those of his soldiers who'd been spared commitment.

'Understood, Herr Oberstleutnant!'

36

It struck Emmerich that, despite his fatigue, his commanding officer had maintained his poise even in defeat. But it also appeared that he had been willing to accept ignominy rather than be responsible for more pointless bloodshed.

'Then you should know that I have reached an arrangement with the commander of the Maquis. We have agreed that both our forces shall quit the village at the same time. The French will go to the west and we to the east, as far as the Château d'Aubigny.' There he paused, giving his second-in-command a few seconds to assimilate the implications in what he had said. He went on, 'I want you to understand that there must be no thought of pursuing the French Maquis or of our forces reoccupying this village. Now! Do you, as commander of the remaining armed troops, agree to such an arrangement?'

Faced with the decision, it was Emmerich's turn to hesitate. But, then, as he glanced over the huddled mounds in blood-drenched field grey uniforms dotting the meadow amongst the flat black scars of the mortar bombardment, he shouted back, 'Under these circumstances, Herr Oberstleutnant, I am compelled to agree to such an arrangement!'

Overath was seen to glance behind him before answering, as though seeking confirmation from somebody out of sight.

'Then all that remains is for you to send forward your liaison officers, Herr Major!' he said.

Chapter Two

When preliminary reports of the incident at Talmont-les-deux-Ponts reached General Friedel von Sahlenburg, Commander-in-Chief of the St-Etienne Region of the Unoccupied Zone, he hit the ceiling.

He immediately summoned Oberstleutnant Lothar Overath and his Second-in-Command, Major Karl-Heinz Emmerich, to St Etienne and broke all security regulations by telephoning General Klaus-Dieter Elsener, Commander of the 32nd Panzer Division Waffen SS Uber Alles, temporarily laagered within the boundaries of that same region.

General Elsener, together with the commander of his 3rd Panzergrenadier Regiment, Obersturmbannfuhrer Otto Lutz, had already picked up limited Intelligence on the 603rd Infantry Battalion's involvement with the Franc Tireurs et Partisans which he, and his aides, had discussed at some length and with some speculation. In five years of war this was the first report of an irregular French Resistance group humiliating a German infantry unit in battle. The news was undoubtedly grim. Particularly if the 603rd Battalion was representative of the kind of formations now being mustered at short notice in Berlin. After all, the Wehrmacht's war was not with French civilians, but with the Allied armies pouring across the Channel and through beachheads now firmly established along the Cotentin Peninsula of Normandy.

It was, therefore, with a wry smile that General Klaus-Dieter Elsener reacted to the information that General Friedel von Sahlenburg was at the other end of the civilian telephone line.

The Uber Alles Division of the Waffen SS had been mustered in Berlin in December 1939 during the era of the 'phoney war'. Whilst deployed for some months in the manning of the Siegfried Line, the division became prominent in the invasion of Yugoslavia where, as a motorised formation, it was employed in a mobile role to quell local riots and disturbances instigated by guerilla organisations under the command of General Tito.

From Yugoslavia the division was transferred to the rapidly developing Eastern Front where the Wehrmacht was engaged in an all-out offensive towards Moscow, with the intention of finishing off the Russians with the speed and certainty with which they had dealt with the Allies in Belgium, France and Holland. But Hitler had not heeded Napoleon's lesson in respect of the Russian winter, and in the Red Army's counter-offensive, German spearheads facing Moscow were blunted and turned back with crippling casualties. Amongst these, the Uber Alles Division which had been foremost in the drive eastwards and last in the rearguard westwards, was decimated to such a degree that in January 1941 the shattered remnants were sent back to the Fatherland, where they were reformed and regrouped as an armoured division in the SS Panzer Korps.

Four months later, after an ambitious training programme on Luneburg Heath and subsequently in the Austrian Alps, the division was posted back to the Russian Front where, as the war progressed, the Red Army was getting stronger and more experienced in panzer warfare. Dnepropetrovsk, the large industrial town and communications centre on the Dnieper, changed hands several times, with the Uber Alles Division again doubling in the role of spearhead and rearguard as the tide of battle fluctuated across the frozen steppes.

It was a further eighteen months later, however, in the winter of 1943, that the endless battles and privations of the Eastern Front again brought the now-famous Uber Alles Division to its knees. And, once again, its few but dedicated survivors were repatriated to Germany for reformation and reinforcement.

But at this stage of the war, with the Wehrmacht sprawled over most of Europe and with priorities along an 'Iron Coast' reaching from the Spanish border to the north of Norway, there were no longer the class of recruits available which, hitherto, had been specially earmarked for the SS regiments. It subsequently transpired that, by the end of that year, a good twenty per cent of the Waffen SS were not even German nationals, but men who had been recruited with an offer of 'The Full Rights of German Nationality' from the occupied countries which included Alsace-Lorraine, Belgium, Luxembourg and Holland.

This lack of suitable manpower hindered recruitment to the Uber Alles Division as it had been originally planned by Oberkommando Wehrmacht and, reputedly, by Heinrich Himmler himself. As a result, on once again reaching its war establishment strength, the division was posted to the Department of Perigord where new panzer training grounds had been prepared in anticipation of the Allied thrust across the Channel.

There, the command of the division was assumed by SS Oberfuhrer Klaus-Dieter Elsener who was promoted to brigadefuhrer on his appointment.

It was in March 1944, shortly after the arrival of Elsener, that the Uber Alles Division was regrouped and its infantry contingent of two panzergrenadier regiments – the Hess and the Bormann – each of three newly-equipped battalions, were deployed tactically about the region.

The brief to the division was simple and to the point: to protect and maintain routes of communication from the south coast of France to whatever battlefields the Allied invasion of Europe dictated. This meant that during the waiting days the division's prime responsibility was to patrol the region under its jurisdiction and suppress any French Resistance units which either sprang up within the region or had entered from the Occupied Zone as raiding parties.

The Uber Alles panzergrenadier regiments very quickly established for themselves a reputation for cruelty and atrocities towards a civilian population which had had no experience of SS methods. Yet, it soon became apparent to these unfortunate people that the soldiers who perpetrated them must have had special training in this work and, as a result, they withdrew into themselves. The Maquis, inflamed at such treatment of innocent people, stepped up their fight against the SS military formations.

Thus, the atrocities in which the Uber Alles grenadiers still persisted had a self-defeating effect, for the Maquis became all the more determined to provide the invading Allied armies with more indirect support five hundred kilometres south of the Normandy battlefront. Thus, the maxim was born to each and every man of the Franc Tireurs et Partisans: 'Kill-a-Boche-a-Day!'

Immediately the division received official confirmation of the Allied landings in the Baie de la Seine, they reformed to fulfil their pre-allocated role in hurrying to the Allied bridgeheads and eliminating any resistance which they might encounter on the way. The order to march was issued from Generalfeldmarschall Erwin Rommel's headquarters and included instructions to join Army Group B with as little delay as possible. The division's armoured fighting vehicles – the Panzer Mk V Panthers and the Panzer Mk VI Tigers – were to be transported by rail, for these were desperately needed to complete a highly mobile strategic reserve in depth, capable of eliminating any Allied armoured thrusts which managed to break through the defence screen around the bridgeheads.

It also followed that the British Special Operations Executive and General de Gaulle's Bureau d'Action et Résignments would keep the Resistance informed of any such large-scale German movement orders. In consequence, sabotage of the French railways became a top priority.

With the panzers out of the way, the two panzergrenadier regiments of the 32nd Panzer Division Waffen SS Uber Alles – the Hess and the Bormann – began their long road journey northwards. They used motorised infantry vehicles, staff cars, motorcycles and a number of light armoured fighting vehicles. Their panzers were restricted to the Panzer IV model which had originally been used in the 1940 breakthrough into France, but had now been developed with a 268hp Maybach diesel engine, two 7·92mm machine guns and a 75mm gun which equalled the American 76mm anti-tank weapon. These were supported by schutzpanzerwagens with which they planned to pursue any would-be intercepting French Resistance forces across country to their extermination. It followed, too, that the panzergrenadiers would step up their campaigns of terror against the civilian population to discourage any direct support to Maquis bands engaged in destroying railway bridges or ambushing road convoys. But, by this time, the 'Kill-a-Boche-a-Day' campaign was fast gaining momentum and, spurred on by the Allied military successes in the Caen area, the degree of Maquis commitment increased rather than dwindled.

In consequence, the military oppression of French civilians was wholly approved by Oberkommando Wehrmacht and Generalfeldmarschall Wilhelm Keitel issued orders to General Friedel von Sahlenburg, commander of the St Etienne region to that effect. He, in turn, passed them along to Obersturmbannfuhrer Otto Lutz, Commanding the 3rd Regiment of Panzergrenadiers Hess.

A part of these orders, which covered the problems of increasing unrest amongst civilians in the Massif Central region, stated that the population must be made to understand that support to wandering bands of Maquis could only result in a great deal of anguish to themselves. The orders concluded with a direct command that the utmost severity must be employed in dealing with civilians suspected of supporting Maquis-inspired action against German troops or their equipment.

So it was, on the afternoon of the second day following the battle between the Franc Tireurs et Partisans and the German 603rd Infantry Battalion at Talmont-les-deux-Ponts, that General Klaus-Dieter Elsener, commanding the 32nd Panzer Division Waffen SS Uber Alles together with Obersturmbannfuhrer Otto Lutz, commanding the 3rd Panzergrenadier Regiment of that same division, drove to Oberkommando Headquarters, St Etienne.

There they shared a late but relaxed lunch with Regional Commander Friedel von Sahlenburg, in a newish building in the centre of the city which, hitherto, had been the municipal offices. Throughout the lunch they chatted at length of run-of-the-mill problems: the distribution of rations to the civilian population in rural areas; the shortage of fuel for staff cars and trucks used solely on regional administrative work; and, towards the end of the meal, the need for a much higher level of recruitment to second-line support battalions now being posted to Vichy France in increasing numbers. Infantry battalions such as the 603rd!

During lunch, that was the only reference to the 603rd. But, some two hours later, after von Sahlenburg and his guests had adjourned to a small conference room along the corridor, they found that Oberstleutnant Lothar Overath and his second-in-command, Major Karl-Heinz Emmerich, had been waiting there for some time.

They were then joined by two young SS officers whom von Sahlenburg introduced as Sturmbannfuhrer Kurt Bucholz and Hauptsturmfuhrer Jurgen Schroeder. These officers were so much alike in appearance that they could easily have been mistaken for brothers: tall and rangy, fair-haired, blue-eyed, and both with the inbred arrogance of the SS — blatantly apparent in their condescending attitude towards their Wehrmacht seniors, Overath and Emmerich. Both Bucholz and Schroeder wore the insignia of the Iron Cross, 1st Class.

'These boys served with me around Dnepopetrovsk in 1941,' von Sahlenburg said, reflexively fingering his own *Deutsche Kreuz* as he turned to address Elsener and Lutz. 'I've had a hell of a job to get them back on my Staff. Developed into a personal scrap with Rommel in the end! However . . .' He smiled without humour. 'Here they are, so you can guess I had to pull a few strings, eh?'

After that, von Sahlenburg wasted no time. He pitched into the two Wehrmacht officers responsible for the débacle at Talmont-les-deux-Ponts with the sarcasm and fury of a sergeant-major dressing down recalcitrant private soldiers. He made it clear that this was by no means a part of a Court of Inquiry or even a short-circuit to one. A full investigation would follow as quickly as one could be convened and, in the meantime, the two officers could consider themselves under house arrest pending a series of serious charges. Throwing down arms in the face of the enemy! Lacking courage and leadership! Inability to command troops in the field of battle! Each of these could carry a penalty of death by firing squad. Such was the extent of their failure! Unprecedented in the history of the German nation! How would the great German soldiers of yesteryear have reacted to such cowardice, to such flagrant desertion of duty?

During the whole of this condemnation, von Sahlenburg's voice thundered across the narrow confines of the room with the four SS officers little more than an audience to his outrage. Eventually, he turned to them and spread out his hands in a gesture of hopelessness, before ringing for his adjutant to escort the pale-faced and elderly officers of the 603rd Infantry Battalion from the room.

To both Elsener and Lutz it was apparent that the tirade had been so much play-acting on the part of the St Etienne regional commander, who'd simply been going out of his way to emphasise his compliance with Keitel's orders concerning civilian involvement with the Resistance. This also indicated to them that neither he, nor his two new SS boys, wanted any more a part of the Talmont-les-deux-Ponts incident than did the 32nd Panzer Division.

43

Even so, it did suggest that they were going to be left with the rough end of the stick. Of course, with the panzers already speeding north by rail, there was no chance at all of the division being detailed for a major role against the Franc Tireurs et Partisans. But it could be that a detachment of panzergrenadiers still laagered in the region could be made to ensure that the villagers of Talmont-les-deux-Ponts, at least, couldn't give direct support to the Maquis and expect to get away unscathed! Well! All right! An involvement on such a minor scale was fair enough, they'd see to the civilians. As for the Communist-inspired Franc Tireurs et Partisans, they'd be brought to justice soon enough, not by the German military machine but by the Gestapo — who'd already been briefed to that effect!

During the return journey, Klaus-Dieter Elsener sat back comfortably in the back seat of the Mercedes-Benz staff car with his body relaxed and his mind contented. The small doubts which had niggled him during the outward journey had vanished with the knowledge that von Sahlenburg had no intention of seeking permission from Generalfeldmarschall Keitel for the 3rd Panzergrenadier Regiment to be retained in the St Etienne region until the Franc Tireurs et Partisans *réseau* had been eliminated. So, so far as he was concerned, he could forget about the Talmont incident and, along with the rest of his Staff, catch a fast train to Rommel's headquarters at Army Group B. Von Sahlenburg, like Rommel, had had the perspicacity to see where his priorities lay!

Obersturmbannfuhrer Otto Lutz was equally satisfied with the result of the day's briefing. For neither was he likely to be retained in the region. As commander of the 3rd Panzergrenadier Regiment he would detail one company from one of the two battalions and give them a free hand to put the screws on Talmont-les-deux-Ponts. One further satisfying aspect of this assignment was that there was no urgency about it. Whilst he deplored the shambles of the 603rd he was, at the same time, aware of the problems which had been thrust upon its commanders. Even sympathetic. In the first place there had been no Oberkommando Wehrmacht brief concerning the involvement of French Resistance *réseaux* in the area and, clearly, none had been suspected. As a result, Overath had carried out normal security precautions when he should have been alerted to a full war footing. Had this been done, they would have had more chance of squashing the uprising before it had had the time to gather momentum. As it was, their battle had been lost before a shot was fired! What chance had they had against veteran guerilla fighters in a terrain which had obviously been selected because of its ideal defensive topography?

Could the SS have done any better under these circumstances?

Lutz shrugged to himself as the car sped through the rich countryside with its windows wound down and the cooling breeze fanning his face.

Perhaps...

But one thing was certain – they'd have had more than their share of casualties considering the size and military importance of the objective! And that didn't make for good leadership in anybody's book.

Forty-eight hours later, Number 2 Company of the 2nd Battalion of the 3rd Waffen SS Panzergrenadier Regiment Hess halted three kilometres south-east of the village of Talmont-les-deux-Ponts.

In command of the force was Number 2 Company Commander, Hauptsturmfuhrer Horst Kaser, and accompanying him in the role of observer was the 2nd Panzergrenadier Battalion Commander, Sturmbannfuhrer Gunter Haller – at twenty-eight and despite his seniority, three years Kaser's junior.

Haller was present because Obersturmbannfuhrer Otto Lutz had decided that the assignment warranted the overall supervision of an officer of field rank. This last-minute decision was a gesture towards von Sahlenburg rather than anything else, because only that morning the regional Gestapo, by way of Wehrmacht Intelligence, had reported that the Franc Tireurs et Partisans *réseau* had gone to ground. This meant that as the SS panzergrenadiers drove upon Talmont, the Frenchmen who had engaged the 603rd Infantry Battalion there were back home at their farms, workshops, garages and offices and that a good five days would have to elapse before they could be re-mustered once more as a fighting force.

Thus, neither Sturmbannfuhrer Haller, nor any of his battalion officers, anticipated interference so far as the French Resistance was concerned. There was, of course, always the odd lunatic who'd crouch on top of a haystack with a sniper's rifle at his shoulder and knock off German soldiers riding road convoys, but such fanatics had always been a hazard in both the Occupied and the Unoccupied Zones. The troops had learned to live with them and to retaliate with machine guns at the first signs of an ambush.

Haller, Kaser and his three platoon officers sauntered leisurely to the head of the column where two motorcycle scouts were sitting astride their heavy BMW machines with the engines throbbing, weaving heatwaves. The riders pulled their exhaust valve levers as the officers approached and the engines spluttered into silence.

Directly ahead lay the sandstone buildings of Talmont-les-deux-Ponts, viewed from much the same angle as Major Karl-Heinz Emmerich had been presented with two days earlier. But now there was no threat. The tall grasses waving in the summer breeze and the twin parallel lines of willows and alders which marked the flow of the Loze river contained no hidden machine guns. No longer were there Maquis lurking in the thick undergrowth with their fingers on their triggers and their eyes focused through ring and bead sights. Today was more of an outing than a military operation. They would make the German point of view very clear to these villagers without any risk to themselves. It was just another detail.

Five minutes later the column moved on.

Not counting the motorcycles and staff car, there were nine vehicles in all: three Mk IV panzers; three schutz-panzerwagens; and three infantry transporters. The schutzpanzer-wagens and the transporters each carried their complement of grenadiers wearing camouflage dress and carrying full battle equipment, including 7·92mm self-loading rifles G-41 (M); MP-40 9mm Schmeiser Parachutist's maschinen pistoles; and 7·92mm MG-42 machine guns. High-explosive, smoke, and phosphorous grenades were distributed amongst the sections.

As the column turned off the lane, which at that point skirted the Loze river, into a wider road leading to the main east bridge of the village, the point motorcyclists halted. There, they shoved their machines into the rough grass across the verges to make way for the three Mk IV Panzers which edged through their gears to head the column with their 268hp Maybach engines thumping and snorting. The hatches were

46

open and their two 7·92mm machine guns and the long-barrelled 75mm guns were ranged on the distant buildings.

Meanwhile, the rest of the company deployed with the three schutzpanzerwagens close behind the panzers, whilst the Mercedes-Benz staff car took up a position in the column some forty metres behind the panzers from which Haller and Kaser could observe their progress in operational bounds up to the bridge. The point panzer had already sped along the straight stretch of road, the other two covering and moving much slower. Three hundred metres short of the river the leading panzer ran into a hull-down position to the right of the road, whereupon the second panzer accelerated to take over the point until it, too, halted less than fifty metres from the bridge.

The third panzer moved forward very slowly, feeling its way over the *pavé*. The commander was perched high in his turret with binoculars to his eyes, seemingly relaxed, but those who knew the drill realised he had a hand on the smoke mortar plunger and was prepared to duck into the steel plating at the first threat of armed resistance.

As the distance closed he observed civilians strolling along the shaded riverside walk beneath the lines of tall elms edging the bank. There were also young children, barefooted and stripped to the waist, playing on narrow sandy beaches beside the slow-moving current. His brow cleared and he spoke hurriedly into his throat microphone, in instant contact with the signaller at Haller's staff car.

'Hello, Sunray! This is Sunray One! Path clear into village. Everything appears normal. Am proceeding!'

The signaller passed the message to Haller who, with Kaser, settled back to watch the leading Mk IV panzer negotiate the sharp turn on to the incline of the bridge, whilst the two support panzers maintained their hull-down positions with their armament trained on the approach roads and dominating buildings which could house anti-tank weapons.

The panzer mounted the bridge at a crawl with the commander finding time to turn and take in an all-round view. Those at the rear of the column could now also see that there were women and children in the street, whilst more people poured out of the houses to find out what the commotion was about. The panzer moved carefully amongst them from the bridge, the commander waving and smiling into the crowd which was congregating along the riverside walk, in much the same way

47

as when the 603rd Infantry Battalion had first entered the village ten days earlier. But this time there were none of the catcalls which had greeted the infantrymen. With a feeling of apprehension, the villagers noticed more panzers down the road from the bridge, as well as half-tracked vehicles and covered transporters which could only be bringing soldiers.

A stench of burnt timber still hung heavy over the village, whilst from behind the line of houses bordering the river there came the din of men busy tearing down the crumbled shells of the *mairie* and the Auberge de la Bobotte. Tractors towing heavy farm trailers were trundling the débris away for dumping to the north of the village. It was apparent that the people of Talmont-les-deux-Ponts were anxious to remove signs of the recent conflict as quickly as possible.

It was equally apparent they were not going to be allowed to forget the German 603rd Infantry Battalion whose graves scarred the turf of the open ground beyond the schoolhouse. These new arrivals with their panzers, half-tracks and lorried infantry were of a different calibre to the men of the 603rd and there was something about the way they had approached the village in attack formation which spoke of their operational discipline. And that was before any of them had got sufficiently close to identify the Waffen SS insignia on their helmets and epaulettes, or the distinctive cuff-titles of the Uber Alles Division.

The three panzers spaced themselves out along the riverside walk, one mounting guard at each of the two bridges and the third stationed midway between them at the junction with the Rue Gondin. Behind came the three schutzpanzerwagens, which took up supporting positions when heavily armed soldiers leapt out and immediately began to herd the villagers down the street to the Place Gondin. The lorried infantry debussed at pre-selected points on the outskirts of the village, where they sealed off the roads and then they, too, began to push people into the square ahead of them.

Meanwhile, more soldiers had entered the Place Gondin and were directing the villagers on to the Parc des Sports, an area of open parkland bordered on three sides by trees and by the Bar Au Parc Des Sports and its *jeu-de-boule* on the other.

'Identity check!' an officer announced. 'All bring your papers with you! Identity check!'

The crowd in the Parc des Sports began to thicken, mainly

48

with women and children and the few of the men who had so far been rounded up from their work in the Place Gondin. Those who had had experience of the SS knew that today's show of force was following an all too familiar pattern. First they would surround the village; then they would occupy the principal offices such as the police station, the municipal offices and commercial centre. Finally, they would round up the civilian population in double quick time – just as they were doing now!

The increasing aggression of the grenadiers was being witnessed by those who had not yet left their homes as elderly people, who had difficulty in moving quickly enough for the SS, were jostled along with blows from rifle butts about their heads and shoulders. Many of them dropped fainting to the ground, their wounds welling blood as they sprawled in the road.

Young Michel Ferrain, horrified at the brutal treatment of seventy-six-year-old Jules Guedon, shoved aside the young SS-man and stooped over the whimpering Guedon, cradling the frail shoulders in his arms, knowing that if the old man didn't find sufficient strength to move himself he'd be murdered where he lay. But as the grenadier recovered his balance, he swung the muzzle of his Schmeiser machine pistol towards Ferrain and killed him with a single shot.

Its sudden crack rang around the ancient buildings and a stunned silence descended upon the villagers – for now they realised that this was to be no routine identity check. The Waffen SS had come to Talmont-les-deux-Ponts for one reason only – to even up the score for the 603rd Infantry Battalion.

The women crossed themselves and drew their children closer to them. They'd known all along that the Boches wouldn't let the Franc Tireurs et Partisans get away with such an easy victory. Somebody had to pay – and they were the helpless people who'd had to stay on at the scene of the German humiliation.

Seventeen-year-old Solange Duprez was on her way home from Pouroux's bakery across the east bridge with half-a-dozen loaves of crisp, sweet-smelling, fresh bread cradled in her arms. She had come by way of the Rue Tarrant where she had called upon her old schoolfriend, Annette Penard, and knew nothing of the arrival of SS panzergrenadiers in the village. She was a pretty girl, dark-haired, blue-eyed and with a wide smiling mouth with full lips which, with her suntan, did much towards setting off her startlingly white teeth. She was tall, too. Tall and lean, with a pair of ripe breasts which shifted tantalisingly beneath the sheer white cotton of her summer dress.

It was as she emerged from the narrow Rue Tarrant into the open space of the Place Gondin that she bumped head-on into Sturmann Wolfgang Steyr's rifle section. She recoiled, pushing out the bread in front of her to avoid physical contact, her face paling, eyes starting, her mouth forming a round 'O'.

She noticed that several of the soldiers were carrying uncorked bottles of cognac and there was a sharp brightness about their eyes which spelled danger. At once she spun on her heels, striding out to run back the way she had come, but one of Steyr's men reached out and grabbed her arm. Initially, this had been no more than a reflex action on the man's part, but when he paused to look over the prize in his grasp his hold on her tightened. Another soldier shoved his hand between the loaves and her body, cupping the deliciously yielding breast beneath the thin material. And when she screamed it was the signal for Steyr and his section to begin their aggression towards the civilian population of Talmont-les-deux-Ponts in earnest.

They half-carried the screaming, struggling, Solange up the stairs of the nearest house, already deserted. There, they tossed her on to the bed and tied her wrists and ankles to each of the four corners of the heavy wooden bedstead using their equipment straps. Then they stood around the bed, laughing and swigging cognac.

One said, 'Go on, Sturmann! You first!' At which Wolfgang Steyr leaned over the girl and with thumb and forefinger delicately lifted the hem of her skirt to her waist, revealing her long, suntanned legs and the white lace edging to her panties.

'Pull 'em down for her, Sturmann!'

'No! Let's see her tits, first!'

Steyr looked round the group grinning back into the grinning faces, rubbing a hand down the front of his pants showing his erection thrusting hard and against the rough uniform material. Others gulped at their cognac, senses already inflamed at this unexpected piece of good luck which had come their way.

'Jesus! But I'm coming already!' Baumer yelled and he wrenched open his fly with one hand, hauling out his penis and tearing open the girl's blouse with the other hand as he poured his semen copiously over her naked nipples.

The rest roared with laughter, but a new tension had come into all of them.

'The sturmann goes first!'

This was Steyr, himself, and he pulled down her knickers with all the delicacy he had shown when he had lifted her skirt. He rubbed a hand over her triangle of black hair.

'You fellers might as well go for a walk,' he said. 'I plan to take my time!'

But they all cheered as he mounted her, shreiking out in unison the count of his thrusts: '*Eins*! *Zwei*! *Drei*! *Vier*! *Funf*! . . .'

During the next twenty minutes they took her in turn, drinking their cognac and trying to keep down their tensions until their turn came, as they watched their mates pour themselves into the girl's body. Now she had ceased struggling and lay limp, flat on her back, her head turned to the wall, her breasts and buttocks running with semen, her flesh inflamed by the kneading of coarse hands.

As they left her, still tied to the bed, one of the grenadiers turned to Steyr, evidently thinking about the long, avenging arm of the Maquis.

'Didn't we ought to finish her off, Sturmann?'

But Steyr laughed as he shook his head.

'What the hell! It's a hot afternoon. We might want to come back!'

Sixty-nine-year-old Emilie Chevasse had had a moderately serious stroke a couple of weeks earlier which had taken her speech and left her paralysed down the right side of her body. As a result, her seventy-four-year-old husband, Henri, had had to take over the household chores as well as attend to his invalid wife, who was now confined to her bed.

Henri was washing up the lunchtime dishes in their small cottage on the short-cut to the riverside walk – the Rue Rapide – when the SS burst into his kitchen.

'Out! Identity check! Out! Out!'

Henri stared wild-eyed at the Germans, dumbly lifting a hand running with soap suds to indicate the bedroom above. But the SS had no time to waste. Not on old men! Two of them

51

grabbed him by the shoulders and half-carried him to the door and hurled him out on to the road where he collapsed into an untidy heap, barely conscious. And when the SS, impatient now, doubled upstairs and found old Emilie fainting in her bed at the commotion, they ran the bed on to the balcony and tipped her, mattress and all, on top of her husband.

Within half-an-hour over four hundred people had been crammed into the Parc des Sports and divided into two groups: men and women. The women stared across the few metres separating them with tears flooding their cheeks and anguish in their eyes. Meanwhile, SS details of section strength had left the park to move back into the village, where they systematically began to loot the houses, the shops and the bars, stocking up the schutzpanzerwagens with wine, cognac, food and any household things which took their fancy.

The villagers listened pale-faced to the row they made, many of the grenadiers already falling drunk as they pillaged the houses. They also had a gramophone amplified through the loud-hailer system of one of the schutzpanzerwagens churning out non-stop jazz which, ironically, stirred a ray of hope within the villagers. In their desperation, they seized upon this hope, even finding the spirit to speculate.

So they were going to lose a few personal belongings? All right! So what? The war was almost over, anyway, and one day there would be government compensation for all. Losing a few belongings was better than reprisals, wasn't it? And as for the looting of the bars and shops, well, they'd all club together and help make up the owners' losses. They'd still be just as much a family community when the SS had gone as they'd always been!

It was a column of black smoke threading lazily into the clear afternoon sky which caused them to have their doubts. There followed a second! A third! A fourth! *Mon dieu*! Ten and more! The Boches were setting fire to the houses!

The men stared helplessly at their captors, who ringed the group with legs braced and fingers on the triggers of their weapons. Some of the older women fell weeping to their knees, praying, until the SS stalked amongst them and prodded them to their feet with the points of their bayonets.

Minutes later the women were led from the Parc des Sports.

'Move! Move!' The soldiers yelled and shoved them along with their rifles, prodding the children after them until the frantic mothers gathered them into their arms and ran to the head of the procession, near to swooning at the prospect of what might lie ahead. At this, the men surged forward towards the SS troopers in one concerted heave, but the Germans stood their ground and fired bursts from their MP-40 Schmeiser machine pistols over their heads, the bullets pinging off the roman-tiled roof of the Bar Au Parc des Sports.

It was then that the Mercedes-Benz staff car, which had been parked along the Rue Dominique leading to the Place Gondin, crept slowly across the park to where the men were assembled. As it braked, so the SS-men moved amongst their prisoners and rapidly formed them into double lines.

The women and children were turning amongst the buildings as two SS officers climbed from the staff car: a sturmbannfuhrer and a hauptsturmfuhrer. Side by side they sauntered across the open space to where two junior officers were standing.

'How many do we have?' This was the sturmbannfuhrer speaking. 'Enough, I hope!'

The untersturmfuhrers saluted.

'More than enough, sir!' one of them replied promptly. 'A total of a hundred and ninety-eight!'

'Good!'

Sturmbannfuhrer Gunter Haller stepped forward a couple of paces and bleakly looked over the parallel lines of Frenchmen. It struck him they were mostly old men. Perhaps the average age could be around fifty. Even so, his experience with the Resistance in Northern France had proved that an elderly man was equally capable of operating a machine gun as was one half his age. What was more, they invariably handled them with more guts and determination! Age had nothing at all to do with urban guerilla warfare.

'Now listen, you!'

He raised his voice to address them in French. 'You don't have to be told why we're here or what we've come to do. Two days ago, fifty-three German soldiers were assassinated in this village. Fifty-three! And why? Because their commander had the heart to treat you with more leniency than he should have. There should be no leniency for terrorists who hide behind women and children! And now there is to be none for you who allowed that to happen. For every German soldier murdered here, two Frenchmen will die! One hundred and six of you will be executed by firing squad and your bodies will be hung from lampposts, trees and balconies so that others will see the kind of penalty that murderers have to pay! The rest will be dumped in the river with the rats and other vermin! Those of you lucky enough to be spared will then have a chance to let your Communist friends of the Franc Tireurs et Partisans know what has happened. Then, perhaps, in future, you and others might not be so eager to co-operate.'

Hoarse cries of alarm arose at once from the Frenchmen, but they were shouted into silence by the SS, who ran along the ranks wielding rifles and bayonets. The cries subsided and a few old men amongst them who had collapsed on to the grass were kicked to their feet as Hauptsturmfuhrer Horst Kaser with his Company Hauptsturmfuhrer, Walter Muller, came forward.

It was easy enough selecting those who had to die – roughly a half. One or two either way didn't matter so long as the overall number was large enough for justice to be seen to be done and sufficient to appease von Sahlenburg's outrage at Oberkommando Regional Headquarters, St Etienne.

Kaser stared into their haggard faces dispassionately as he strolled leisurely along the front rank. In the battalion mess there had recently been a line of talk that Resistance fighters were dirty, scruffy characters who were too involved in ambushing unsuspecting Germans to keep themselves clean and presentable. Kaser knew that this was no more than idle chatter but, at least, it would serve as a yardstick to decide on who should live and who should die. So, languidly, he pointed out the men who had not shaved or whose clothes were work-soiled, or whose shoes were scuffed and worn.

The hauptscharfuhrer behind him bawled at them as they were selected, 'One pace forward. Move!'

The men shambled forward with ashen faces and eyes turned towards the exit from the park where their womenfolk had disappeared. Identity check, the officer had said – and they'd been stupid enough to believe him! Now it was too late – even to have a last look at their wives and mothers.

The hauptscharfuhrer separated the condemned from the spared at a distance of some twenty metres and Kaser strolled between the two groups, glancing from one to the other.

I'm seeking volunteers!' he announced. 'I need men keen to decorate the village with a few dead bodies! They can pick

54

their own places.' He lifted his eyebrows at the stunned silence which followed, then swung round quickly on those who had been spared. 'Is there to be no reaction from you lucky ones?'

None moved and Kaser looked across the grass to grin at Haller who was watching from the edge of the park.

Then he focused his attention on the other group.

'Then how about you men? Don't you realise you'll be dead within a half-hour? How about swapping places with some of the happy men over there? Look! Here's a deal! I'll switch places with every man amongst you who volunteers for the hanging!'

Gasps of shock came from both groups, though all were aware that this SS-captain was playing with them. But it could also be a last chance to go on living – even though a man would have to face his conscience, and his friends, after the deal had been struck.

Eventually it was Emil Leboeuf who pushed himself forward from the group to be spared. He was about forty-five-years-old, a big man with powerful shoulders and a complexion fiery-red from a life out of doors. His head was erect as he addressed Kaser in tones loud enough for all to hear.

'I will help with the hanging if you will spare my son, sir!' He pointed distractedly into the group of the condemned. 'He is not yet seventeen. Afterwards, you can hang me!'

A silence followed. There was not a Frenchman there who did not recognise the poignancy of Leboeuf's plea. They knew that his wife had died only weeks earlier during a late childbirth and that the poor man lived only for his son.

Kaser looked at Leboeuf, staring into his dark eyes with the same kind of cheerful grin on his face as he had shown to Haller a moment earlier.

'Ah! A good man and no doubt a devoted father. What is your name?

'Leboeuf, sir. Emil Leboeuf!'

'Then tell me, M'sieu Leboeuf, do you love your son?'

Leboeuf nodded.

'I love him with all my heart, sir!'

'Then would it not be cruel for the two of you to be separated?'

Leboeuf's expression relaxed and tears sprang suddenly from his eyes to course uncontrollably down his weatherbeaten cheeks.

'Indeed, it would, sir!'

'Good! Then point me out your son!'

Leboeuf lifted a hand to indicate a tousle-headed boy standing with a group of middle-aged men towards the end of the line opposite him.

He called, 'Step towards the officer, Yves!' and the boy, tall for his age, did as his father bade him.

Kaser looked him over, then turned back to Leboeuf.

'Yes. A fine son of a fine father, *m'sieu*! As I said, the two of you shall not be separated. You can join your son!'

Leboeuf recoiled.

'No! He must join me!'

'Must? Must? What a strange word to use to an SS officer, *m'sieu*. Or don't you think so?'

He motioned to a squad of grenadiers who ran at Leboeuf with fixed bayonets and jabbed him viciously in the buttocks, jostling him across the twenty metres to halt beside his son amongst the men Kaser had appointed to die.

Kaser turned back to the other group.

'Now! Let us have no more of this stupid chatter. Let me see some volunteers come forward and quickly!'

One by one, figures shambled from amongst the group of condemned, eyes averted from those who had chosen to let the SS have their heads.

Kaser counted their numbers out loud and when he reached ten he held up a hand.

Haller and Kaser sought the shade of the striped awning of the Bar Au Parc des Sports under which they lounged in cane chairs, sipping pastis with only a part of their attention on the mass executions being carried out across the way.

Hauptscharfuhrer Walter Muller had detailed four firing squads, each of ten panzergrenadiers, and then split the French hostages into four groups of approximately twenty-five. To each of these he allocated a firing party and marched three of them to the other side of the park from where they could see what was happening to their friends – until their own turn to die came around.

He lined up the first group in single-file with their backs to the concrete wall which was a part of a makeshift grandstand, and the prisoners stood there silently waiting for the inevitable, their eyes clouded with fear and remorse and straying to the castellated square tower of the church where they believed their womenfolk had been taken.

The first fusillade proved this to be so, for with the chatter of the SS machine pistols there arose from the church a concerted hysterical screaming which increased in intensity at the second burst. The third group had a few minutes' respite, clearing away the bodies of the dead to make room for themselves, whilst two SS rottenfuhrers with drawn Luger automatics moved amongst the bleeding bodies finishing off any who, miraculously, still breathed.

The uncontrolled hysteria of the women continued long after the last of the Frenchmen had died, and the SS bolted the church door and fired random bursts through the high windows to make them keep their heads down. Then they rounded up the ten 'volunteers' from the ninety-odd survivors and escorted them to the Place Gondin, where they collected the tractors and trailers used in clearing away the debris from the *mairie* and the Auberge de la Bobotte. These they were made to load with the bodies, whilst others collected coils of rope from the Union Agricole.

At this point, the SS officers seemed to lose interest in the proceedings and the grenadiers still on guard were allowed to stand-down, whereupon they immediately began looting what remained of the drink at the Bar Au Parc des Sports and settled themselves down at vantage points where they could watch the French volunteers go about their hanging detail.

Later, these grenadiers wandered into the deserted streets, shouting obscenities up at the corpses which gyrated back and forth at the end of their ropes and dripped congealing blood on to the pavements. Many snatched up stones which they hurled viciously at the dead Frenchmen, laughing uproariously and pounding each other on the back whenever they scored a new wound in the dead flesh.

They knew they were being retained in the village on the off-chance that the Franc Tireurs et Partisans had been aroused by the afternoon's action and planned to retaliate. Though, at the same time, they believed there could be little chance of this happening. The Maquis were unlikely to stick their necks into a noose as wide as this one! Anyway, they'd be smart enough to spot the Mk IV Panzers and the schutzpanzerwagens on guard at the two bridges and along the river walk where the volunteers, streaming sweat and crumpling in fatigue, were disposing of the last of the dead. By this time night clouds were building up over the village and shadows deepening beneath the trees lining the river, so that the corpses slipped silently and almost unnoticed down the steep banks to disappear beneath the surface with barely a ripple. Only the trails of blood over the pavement marked their last journey from the Parc des Sports to the Loze.

With dusk, Sturmbannfuhrer Gunter Haller and Hauptsturmfuhrer Horst Kaser rose from their chairs. They had dined well from a menu prepared by a grenadier mess cook enhanced by 1932 Chateauneuf du Pape looted from the bar's cellars.

Now they had tired of Talmont-les-deux-Ponts.

They had seen the French hostages hanging from almost every lamppost, balcony and tree in the village centre and Haller, satisfied with the day's work, decided to leave. He and Kaser would drive back to headquarters right away, taking a schutzpanzerwagen as escort. That would be safer than with the full convoy, since officers in staff cars became sitting ducks for roadside snipers who believed that the length of the column was a fair indication of the officer's importance. Besides, there was to be a farewell party in the mess that night and, like every other officer of the 3rd Panzergrenadier Regiment Hess, he didn't want to miss the opportunity of wishing good luck to those who were to leave for Panzer Group B, Normandy, the following day. It would be good for them all to get back into the real war again, and most of those who had served with Uber Alles on the Russian Front would agree with him.

So with the women and children of Talmont-les-deux-Ponts still barricaded in the church and with their cries still plaintively echoing above the din of the amplified jazz, the two officers got into the Mercedes-Benz staff car, leaving the company under the command of a senior platoon officer, Untersturmfuhrer Werner Odermatt.

Von Sahlenburg would be well pleased at the speed and the aggressive manner in which eye-for-an-eye reprisals had been carried out against the civilian population. Similarly, their divisional commander, General Klaus-Dieter Elsener, would be gratified by the knowledge that he could also leave for Normandy in the morning with the slate clean as far as the Maquis were concerned.

All in all, this had been a worthwhile day and that from everybody's point of view!

The 2nd Panzergrenadier Battalion had grasped the opportunity to prove they were ready and able to carry out, efficiently and without comment, any order issued by a senior rank —

an essential attitude for every SS soldier! The mass executions had also helped blood them for the coming battles. Yes, all in all, a good day!

The staff car turned off the Rue Gondin into the riverside walk as the French volunteers were disposing of the last of the corpses. It crossed Haller's mind that as soon as the SS pulled out, these same men would in all probability drag them out again at gunpoint and then face a firing squad of their own countrymen. That was one of the harsh realities of guerilla warfare which all French peasants should have learned as far back as 1939 – long before they'd demonstrated their eagerness to help the Maquis. Could even be that some of the volunteers were also members of the Franc Tireurs et Partisans. That would be a hell of a laugh!

Here and there houses were still burning, for there had been nobody to fight the fires whilst SS grenadiers, clutching looted bottles of cognac, had run in gangs down the streets tossing burning brands from one house to another. To the officers this was a stupid destruction of valuable property, but as von Sahlenburg had insisted, the French bastards had to be taught their lesson.

At the east bridge they picked up the escort schutzpanzerwagen which, with its complement of grenadiers, had been on guard duty during the whole afternoon. These men had seen nothing of what had happened in the Parc des Sports. The noise from the firing squads had caused some comment, but they had shied at investigation. If they had to know, then they would be told by their officers all in good time!

Batiste Couecou ran the ancient Citroen 15 into a belt of trees less than twenty metres from the junction with the Viverois-St Bonnet turn-off and roughly ten kilometres south-east of Talmont-les-deux-Ponts. He doused the lights and he and the other man in the car remained where they were until Armand Guerineau had checked the map.

A couple of minutes went by before Guerineau straightened himself and stretched with a sigh. He looked from Couecou to young François Herbin sitting in the passenger seat. The strain was evident in the boy's face, even in the half-light, as he pointed along the road ahead to where it ran into thicker woodland, where it became absorbed in shadows and a tunnel of foliage.

'That's the place I had in mind,' Guerineau summed up brusquely. 'We'll blow up the half-track amongst the trees. The staff car's got to stop behind it. There's no way it can get off the road!' He lunged forward impulsively to throw open the car door. 'Come, for Christ's sake! We've got little more than a quarter of an hour. Let's get to work on the explosive!'

Most of the executions had already taken place by the time Armand Guerineau learned of the arrival of the SS panzergrenadiers in Talmont-les-deux-Ponts. The information had been telephoned direct to his farm cottage on the outskirts of Puy, and his anger had flared the moment he recognised the voice of Danielle Bouleau.

'Danielle!' He screamed down the phone at the old lady. 'You know better than to ring me here! You've got to use the network, that's what it's ...'

'Listen Armand!'

Her voice rose shrilly above his and the hint of panic crushed him into silence. 'The SS are here in Talmont! Perhaps a hundred of 'em! They've got panzers, half-tracks and machine guns. Already they're marching people to the Parc des Sports and setting fire to the houses. You must do ...'

Guerineau caught his breath, shaking his head, denying the facts as though the woman were standing beside him.

'We're not mobilised, Danielle! You know we stood-down yesterday. The *réseau* cannot risk a confrontation with the SS unless we're wanting to commit suicide. All of us!'

'No! No! No!' Impatience began to take the edge off her panic. 'That's not what I'm saying! I'm telling you the SS are already here! It's too late to stop them! Reprisals have already begun. But we must do something, Armand! Maybe they plan to raze the whole village. Who knows? We can't let the Boches get away with this. Not even the SS!'

'Where are you now, Danielle?'

'At my home, where else? But now I am leaving for the headquarters if I can make it. You understand! I will go to the headquarters and let you know what these morons do next!'

'At the Viverois number, Danielle!'

'But, of course! Now that I have found you!'

That was how Armand Guerineau learned that Sturmbannfuhrer Gunter Haller and Hauptsturmfuhrer Horst Kaser had decided to leave the SS withdrawal from Talmont-les-deux-Ponts under the command of his junior officers – because seventy-eight-year-old Danielle Bouleau had been sufficiently alert to watch them drive away in their Mercedes-Benz staff car behind the schutzpanzerwagen escort. At the time she had quietly crossed herself, lifted her eyes heavenwards, and picked up the telephone.

Guerineau had not wasted a second and by the time he had joined Couecou and Herbin they were standing by in the Citroen, with enough high explosive in the boot to burst open a Mk IV Panzer. Luckily, too, their farmstead to the south of Viverois was not more than half-a-dozen kilometres from the Monistrol-sur-Loire road along which the SS would travel back to their headquarters.

Guerineau had smiled to himself at that. For once, it appeared, Madame Fortune was on the side of the *réseau*!

Now the three men were working together in a tight little group, hacking with spades at the tangled roots which spread beneath the ribbon of tarmacadam. The trench needed to be a full metre deep if the explosion was to blast upwards through the road surface. Time wasn't on their side. Could be they were already down to minutes and their anxiety was demonstrated by the fury with which they splintered the stubborn roots.

'It'll have to do!' Guerineau stood up streaming sweat, a hand at his aching back. 'Let's get out the explosive.'

The others straightened themselves, too, mopping their foreheads with the backs of dirt-ingrained hands as they hurried back to the Citroen, their eyes focused down the straight stretch of road which led back to Talmont-les-deux-Ponts.

They had almost a hundred kilograms of TNT packed into two sacks. It wasn't easy manoeuvring these out of the car boot and it was even more difficult humping them over the rough ground to the trench they'd dug. But once they had been wedged there, Guerineau left his companions pounding stones and soil on top whilst he went back to the car where, from the glove compartment, he took primers, detonators and a spool of double cable.

He worked quickly, opening the bonnet and securing one end of each of the two wires to a hinge and then running out the wires to where Couecou and Herbin were still padding in the explosive.

As he approached they stood aside to give him room to wedge a primer between the two sacks. Gingerly, then, he inserted a detonator into the hollow core of the primer. Couecou handed

61

him small flat stones, one at a time, with which he built a small platform above the detonator. Through one side of this platform he connected the two wires to the detonator terminals, then glanced up at Couecou and spreading out his hands with a wry grin. Despite their haste, it looked as though things could be going their way – providing old Danielle hadn't jumped to the wrong conclusion and the Germans weren't planning to come along this road, anyway!

Couecou shrugged, acknowledging his leader's silent comment, and began to lay soil carefully over the detonator whilst Guerineau again went back to the car where he connected one of the wires to the battery negative terminal. The other he bared for three or four centimetres and hooked it over one of the spark plugs.

Seconds later, Couecou and Herbin joined him. They were breathing hard, but there were smiles of satisfaction on their faces. There was nothing more they could do now. All Guerineau had to do was touch the battery positive terminal with the bared wire and the road in the trees would erupt.

What happened next was up to *le bon Dieu*!

But barely a minute had passed when, along the road from the west, there came the distant grumble of approaching traffic. The Frenchmen stiffened, then slipped deeper into the undergrowth behind the Citroen, Guerineau's eyes flitting from the tunnel into the trees twenty metres distant to the loose wire from the detonator in his hand. The moonlight was too bright, he decided. Had there been time he'd have gone farther down the road to see whether there were reflections glinting from the exposed parts of the car. That was something he should have thought about earlier.

The vehicles were coming hard. Could be there was an armoured scout car ahead of the staff car. They'd not reckoned on that! The plan had been simply to blow up the schutzpanzerwagen and then gun down the staff car driver. Maybe, after all, Danielle Bouleau had got her facts mixed. Maybe old age was taking its toll ... he was on the point of cursing her until he recalled that had it not been for Danielle, the Boches could well have got away with their afternoon's killing. At least, the *réseau* would grab themselves something – even if that was only a staff car with dead men inside it!

Now they could see narrow slits of light from the headlamp masks of what appeared to be the leading vehicle. They were growing brighter with every second. The car was certainly coming at speed.

Guerineau tensed, spacing the gap between the bared wire and the battery positive terminal with the width of a forefinger. All he had to do was time the split-second when the half-track, or whatever it was, drew level with the belt of trees and press down the live wire against the...

He began a mental countdown from ten: nine, eight . . . the leading vehicle was almost level and the wire was millimetres from the battery terminal when he saw that this was no German vehicle but a 1,500cc Renault with civilian registration plates; probably a GP from Viverois or St Bonnet!

He hooked the wire back over the bonnet-hinge and wiped sweat from his steaming face, staring grimly at the silhouttes of Couecou and Herbin deeper in the trees. That had been close, by Christ! Maybe news of the mass executions in Talmont was causing him to become too impulsive. Maybe the undeniable fact that, ultimately, the Franc Tireurs et Partisans had been responsible made those horrific murders all the more personal, all the more necessary to be avenged.

There came the sound of further vehicles approaching from the west. Again, the three men peered into the darkness along that same stretch of road. This was a much heavier vehicle, the engine note told them as much. Or it could be there were more than one, and coming fast, too. Whoever they were, they were conscious of their vulnerability on a dark country road or, equally, they could just be in a hell of a hurry! Whichever! They spelled out Boches and, with that realisation, much of the disillusionment which had begun to haunt Guerineau vanished. Please God they were Boches! Better still, SS. Better still, SS officers. Better still, senior SS officers!

There were two vehicles. Racing towards them, clearly intending to disregard any danger which the belt of trees ahead might be hiding, relying on their speed and latent fire-power to blast their way through any ambush. In this kind of terrain there were too many ambush spots to warrant a reconnaissance of each and every one.

'Half-track!'

Couecou spat the word across the distance to Guerineau who nodded in acknowledgement. He, too, had heard the slap-slap-slap of the leading segments of the tracks clattering down on the road surface before the driving sprocket at the rear snatched up

63

the tension. There was no disguising a half-track on a metalled road, by Christ! Now it all depended on how many vehicles there were in support and which might be leading. Please God old Danielle had been spot on...

His heart bumped. He could make out the square, box-like, construction of a schutzpanzerwagen with its driver and forward gunner sitting high above the front wheels... and there was only one vehicle behind. Just one! It didn't matter a damn who might be inside it any more. They'd be SS and, right now, that was enough!

Their speed had not slackened. They'd spotted the tunnel into the trees and were intent on charging blindly through at maximum revs; the half-track a good three hundred metres ahead of the second vehicle—a car! A Mercedes-Benz staff car!

Thank God! Couldn't be better!

Guerineau got no more than a fleeting glimpse of the schutzpanzerwagen as it raced past him—a mere impression of the bulk of the heavy vehicle and the coal scuttle steel helmets of the panzergrenadiers who lined its open well with their Schmeiser machine pistols held hard against the rim. He was watching the trees ahead and, the instant the half-track hit the shadows across the road, he shoved down the bared wire hard on to the battery positive terminal.

He continued to hold it there even as the roar of the explosion rocked the Citroen and a fireball shot into the air, lighting up the copse bright as day. He caught a glimpse of panzergrenadiers being tossed into the air and sensed a splash against his cheek which he knew must be blood. German blood! But his eyes now were only for the staff car which came skidding frantically past him sideways, tyres screaming, pouring white smoke. He was aware, too, of the crash of grenades as Couecou and Herbin lobbed them accurately into the heap of twisted burning metal which had been a schutzpanzerwagen. As the fuel tank exploded there spurted a second fireball and, in the new light, Herbin rested a British Bren light machine gun across the branch of a tree and leisurely fired in morse the Allied 'V' for Victory signal, in three single shots followed by a burst.

By this time, the staff car had spun wildly into an irrigation ditch across the road and the SS driver had already clambered out. His hands were clasped above his head.

'Stay right there!'

The German lifted his hand higher, as Guerineau turned his

attention to two officers who were having trouble getting through the rear door.

'You too! Stay where you are!'

The officers halted beside their driver. It struck Guerineau they were smiling. As though they hadn't expected this kind of reaction from a detachment of Maquis which wasn't even mobilised.

'It's all right,' one of them replied in even tones. 'We are prepared to accept that we are your prisoners.'

'Toss your sidearms over here where I can see them!'

'We are unarmed.'

'Then your driver!'

'So is he!' the other officer said, pointing at the blazing wreck of the schutzpanzerwagen. 'That was our weapon!'

Herbin joined Guerineau.

'They're all dead, Armand!' he announced. 'We checked, but Robert's making double sure. Most of 'em died in the explosion. The grenades and the Bren did the rest.'

Guerineau nodded and called again to the officers.

'Come over here! Both of you! Hands above your heads. Now! Slowly!'

But Sturmbannfuhrer Gunter Haller and Hauptsturmfuhrer Horst Kaser dug in their heels at that.

'I don't know how many there are of you,' Haller replied brusquely, 'but don't you think you'd better call the half-track your prize and leave it at that?'

'Move! Or I shoot!'

'You wouldn't! We're too valuable to kill out of hand.'

'I only need one of you. Now, move!'

Still they hesitated and Guerineau killed the driver with a single shot. The man spun round under the muzzle velocity of the ·303-inch bullet with an expression of incredulity on his face. Then, as he toppled over, blood gushed from his mouth and splattered on to the road at the officers' feet.

'You on the right! You're to be next! If you want to see just how valuable you are, then try me!'

'Very well!'

There was a hint of insolence in the officer's tone, but Guerineau knew he'd won.

When Couecou rejoined them they bundled the two officers into the back seat of the Citroen and lashed their hands to the door armrests, young Herbin perched between them with the short muzzle of a Schmeiser machine pistol pushed hard against Haller's chest.

Couecou took the wheel and skilfully steered through the wreckage of the still-burning schutzpanzerwagen. Incredibly, the driver and forward gunner, even in death, were still sitting high in their operational positions, as though they might have braced themselves for the explosion. Or it could have been that Guerineau's timing had been spot-on and the explosive charge had hit the half-track just where and when he'd wanted it – under the well where the complement of panzergrenadiers were sitting. In the black fumes billowing around the vehicle lay their bodies, most of them stripped naked by blast, their limbs red with blood and sinew and roasting flesh through which white shafts of bone protruded. The head and torso of one soldier still sprawled across the well where the track had snaked free from the driving sprocket and slashed him in two. Yet his face reflected none of the agony which had been his. His helmet had toppled from his head and his shock of fair hair tumbled over a wide clear forehead, as though the wind had blown it there. But, below, his body terminated at the waist and from the severed trunk there oozed a red-white mix of blood and mucus which dripped into the burning grass, sizzling and spluttering as the heat caught it.

At the other side a grenadier lay slumped against a tree. This soldier had not died from the explosion or the crash, but had been thrown clear by blast when a grenade had exploded across his chest and gouged out most of his ribs, whilst the organs inside hung from a sickening bloody, fleshy mass over the man's belt and equipment.

Couecou shrugged as he caught his leader's eye. At least this made up for some of what had happened that afternoon at Talmont-les-deux-Ponts. This and the two officer bastards they'd got roped up in the back!

Chapter Three

News of the capture of Sturmbannfuhrer Gunter Haller, commanding officer of the 2nd Panzergrenadier Battalion, and Hauptsturmfuhrer Horst Kaser, commanding officer of the 2nd Company, by an unknown *réseau* of the French Resistance put a damper on the officers' farewell party planned to send off the Uber Alles Waffen SS Division to a spirited campaign in Normandy.

By the time the main body of the 2nd Company had left Talmont-les-deux-Ponts and stumbled upon the burned-out schutzpanzerwagen and the abandoned staff car, the trail of the Maquis had iced.

Even so, Untersturmfuhrer Werner Odermatt whom Kaser, prior to his departure with Haller, had put in charge of the company had used his initiative and thrown a ring of armour and grenadiers around the scene of the ambush. Each and every farm and dwelling within a radius of six kilometres had been explored and searched. People had been manhandled into cellars at bayonet point. Women had been stripped naked and children herded into outhouses as an added threat to both parents. But this time there had been neither rape nor arson; not because the SS had suddenly tired of their inbred sport concerning innocent civilians, but because there wasn't the time. Also, a sudden glut of fires over the countryside would have acted as a warning to other Resistance groups – including those who'd taken Haller and Kaser. What the SS needed most of all was time – and luck!

Even so, they achieved nothing.

Odermatt was in constant radio-link with Divisional Headquarters and used the available Intelligence data in pressing on his search for the missing officers, but without success. Subsequently, as the possibility of failure began to take a positive dimension, the officers' party dissolved into little more than a flurry of handshakes amongst junior officers who suddenly found that, so far as their prepared speeches were concerned, they had only half an ear of their seniors.

Toasts were proposed, but hurriedly, and it was the guest of honour, General Friedel von Sahlenburg, Commander-in-Chief of the St Etienne region, who suggested that the party should break up and give the officers concerned an opportunity to direct their full attention to the grave problem which now confronted the 2nd Battalion.

General Klaus-Dieter Elsener, Divisional Commanding Officer, agreed wholeheartedly, sensing that here was a crisis which had hit them out of the blue and which could very well interfere with his personal commitments with Generalfeldmarschall Erwin Rommel at Army Group B.

At the time it had appeared a simple solution to appoint Horst Kaser and his Number 2 Company to nudge the erring villagers of Talmont-les-deux-Ponts. Now he wasn't so sure! And why the hell had Haller and Kaser been so bloody stupid as to tear about the French countryside with a makeshift escort after what had happened that afternoon? The answer, he supposed, was to get to this bloody party!

Incredible!

And now von Sahlenburg had taken the bit between his teeth and wanted to see results — tonight! Of course, Elsener knew that both Haller and Kaser were also old buddies of the general. Along with his recently appointed personal aides, Bucholz and Schroeder, they'd served together a couple of years on the Dneiper Front. There, Haller had been awarded the *Ritterkreuz* and *Kaser*, the Iron Cross Classes 1 and 2 for their part in a sacrificial counterattack which had relieved the Grossdeutschland Division from encirclement by the Red Army.

Bloody fools, all the same! Both of them! Elsener, too, had thought highly of them but, by Christ, this little episode didn't bear thinking about! And von Sahlenburg was thumping the table.

Von Sahlenburg's impatience became all the more apparent the following morning at around seven am when Elsener's servant aroused him from a sleep which had not come easily.

The general sat up in bed, immediately irritable.

'What the hell is it, Kaufmann?'

'Telephone, sir. Personal call from General von Sahlenburg!'

Elsener groaned as he heaved himself out of his bed. He could visualise the regional commander at the other end of the line. The man wouldn't have slept a wink and all night he'd have been fermenting himself into a fury.

Elsener padded across the carpet to his desk beneath the

window, where he snatched back the heavy curtains to scowl out on to a rising heat-mist shrouding the parkland which ran down to the majestic Loire. This could be a good day to move a couple of panzergrenadier regiments, he told himself, clear and still and offering nothing at all to *réseau* snipers and roadside saboteurs.

Damn von Sahlenburg!

He picked up the phone and with the click of the contact points there immediately came a measured, cultured voice rising in the query, 'General Klaus-Dieter Elsener, sir?'

This was evidently one more of von Sahlenburg's aides.

Elsener replied, 'Yes, it is!' and hung on to the receiver.

Seconds later, 'Ah, Klaus!' Von Sahlenburg sounded good-humoured. Elsener pulled a wry face. This was the general's usual ploy when he needed a favour. He went on, 'Not getting you up too early, I hope. I know you've got a full day ahead of you!'

Elsener guessed that von Sahlenburg was sounding out the time he'd fixed for the regiments' departure, but he'd no intention of telling him and he also knew that the regional commander wasn't likely to be so specific over a telephone line.

'It's all laid on, Friedel,' he replied conversationally. 'I've decided to fly, anyway. The feldmarschall wants me up there right now with the panzers.'

'Fly? With the Luftwaffe?'

Elsener laughed.

'With army communications. Feiseler Storch! Otto Lutz will be bringing up the convoy.'

'Ah! Then that simplifies things for me a little. But I still need your help.'

Elsener smiled. He knew full well what the general was seeking, but he asked innocently, 'Help, Friedel?'

'Yes!' The kind of edge which Elsener had expected at the start now came into von Sahlenburg's voice. 'You know, of course, that both Haller and Kaser served with me in Russia? Both were decorated when we sprung the Grossdeutschland boys out of Dnepropetrovsk...'

'Yes, I do! After all, Gunter Haller was one of my senior commanders.'

'Yes! Yes! I was only making the point that I've a personal axe to grind in this kidnapping.'

'So has the division! But what do you expect me to do about it, Friedel? Leave behind a major force to help track down these officers? To deplete a division scheduled for a fighting front

69

which is hourly reported to be getting more involved?'

'I thought, perhaps, one company for a couple of days. No more! Perhaps the company which made its mark at Talmont? Number 2 Company of the 2nd Battalion of your Hess Regiment. They've already earned themselves a reputation. They could put more pressure on French civilians if not on the Resistance! Enough to force the release of Haller and Kaser!'

Elsener took a deep breath and let a couple of seconds go by before answering.

'Just one thing, Friedel,' he asked quietly. 'You, too, have Wehrmacht infantry under your personal command. I cannot possibly divert a detachment from my division to do their work.'

'But you know that my security force is the scrapings of the Wehrmacht! You know the kind of show the 603rd put up at Talmont! The French will ridicule them and, besides, these men have no heart for reprisals. They're good for patrolling street corners and railway crossings, and not even that all the time! I need SS! Uber Alles SS!'

Again Elsener paused before he replied, his voice now cold and brusque. 'I'm sorry, but there's no chance. No chance at all, Friedel!'

'Rommel will understand! If you were to seek from him an authority. He will agree that these are extenuating circumstances and, after all, the war won't be lost because a company of grenadiers is a few days late in arriving at Army Group B. You'll probably find that your whole division is laagered up over that period!'

'Sorry, Friedel!'

'Is that your last word, Klaus?'

'I'm afraid it must be!'

There followed a lengthy pause, but when von Sahlenburg replied his voice had regained some of its earlier good humour.

'Ah, well! The decision must be yours, of course! I appreciate that you'll miss Gunter and Horst as much as I will but, as you say, you have other more involved priorities. So!' He jerked a laugh. 'I wish you a pleasant flight north and good luck in the coming skirmish with the Americans. Look after yourself, Klaus, and see you tip them back into the Channel!'

Elsener smiled, immediately relieved as the problem lifted from his shoulders. Of course, von Sahlenburg had known all along he couldn't hold back a full panzergrenadier company without Rommel's personal approval. He'd just been trying it on!

70

'Thank you, Friedel,' he murmured then. 'You, too! Take care and maybe, before too long, we may also be seeing you around Caen!'

It was at four-thirty that afternoon that the long column of two panzergrenadier regiments – the Hess and the Bormann and each of three battalions – left their St Etienne laager to begin the long haul to join Rommel's Panzer Group B.

The time of departure had been carefully calculated to ensure they reached their overnight laager-zone in the Fôret d'Ivers north of Moulins just as dusk was falling. By that time, the varied units within the regiments' establishment would have formed into one enormous column which, depending upon the nature of the terrain, would have covered some thirteen to fourteen kilometres of highway. Primarily, these would be the 'soft underbelly' of service supply vehicles: stores; ammunition; cooks; medical orderlies; signallers; ordnance engineers; field engineers; mobile bath operators; canteen staff and even field brothels. And, as with a nautical convoy, the speed of a military road convoy was also determined by the speed of the slowest vehicles. Those more likely than not, would be the Mk IV Ausfuhrung Panzers and the schutzpanzerwagen half-tracks, which could have a hell of a problem skidding and sliding over the smooth surfaces of the metalled roads.

The point reconnaissance scout cars would be grimly holding their cruising speed down to forty kilometres an hour but, at the tail of the column, the rearguard would be whipping along at twice or three times that speed. Nothing could be done about it. This was just one of the problems concerning military road convoys which officers had to learn to live with!

Obersturmbannfuhrer Otto Lutz was taking no chances and most of the morning had been spent discussing route procedure at an 'O' Group which had included officers down to untersturmfuhrer rank. He had recapitulated on the worsening situation which had developed with the French Resistance during the past twenty-four hours. Things couldn't have been timed more badly so far as the move was concerned! First the Franc Tireurs et Partisans' attack on the 603rd Infantry Battalion and then the SS reprisals which had had to follow on Keitel's personal command.

Now the Resistance would be wanting to show their teeth again. After what had happened at Talmont-les-deux-Ponts they'd some face to regain – proved by the kidnapping of Haller

71

and Kaser. As Lutz saw it, armed aggression towards the SS and the Wehrmacht was bound to accelerate. The French, both as organised Maquis bands and as odd groups of farmhands with nineteenth-century rifles, would be breaking their necks to take potshots at unsuspecting Germans.

This meant that every grenadier and every serviceman in the column needed to keep his eyes constantly peeled on the surrounding countryside and never, foe one moment, slacken. His weapon must be permanently ready for retaliation with safety catch forward.

As for the by-roads, the scout cars would patrol parallel to the length of the column. They could rely on this highly-mobile element to provide some advance warning to the grenadiers vulnerable in their trucks and half-tracks as well as to the service vehicles.

Immediately behind the point reconnaissance came the fighting tanks, the Mk IV Panzers also deployed operationally with their assault Sturmgeschutz guns trained on alternate sides of the road, the commanders pre-selecting possible ambush points and briefing their gunners to range on them. One problem was that the nose-to-tail convoy, compelled to keep to the main roads, would rarely make it possible for the panzers to swan into the countryside quickly enough, should an emergency suddenly develop.

The Schutzpanzerwagens were dispersed along the length of the convoy together with SdKfz 10/4 half-tracks mounting 2cm flak-guns, which could also be equally effective against armour and ground targets. These, in addition to the schutzpanzerwagens, also carried heavily armed squads of panzergrenadiers, forming a fast-moving strike-force likely to be avoided by small impulsive bands of French guerillas. Organised Maquis would be a different proposition, but the only way to guard against these was by pre-reconnaissance from the air, with a strike-force of fighter-bombers which could be committed even before the ground forces came into the action.

General Klaus-Dieter Elsener watched the 3rd Panzergrenadier Regiment form up into column of route before he climbed aboard the single-engined Storch multi-purpose communications aircraft. Airborne, it still looked impressive, but also highly vulnerable. He would have given much to have been looking down on to that same scene from a Focke Wulf Fw-189 with its twin engines and four 7·92mm heavy machine guns, and knowing there were more squadrons standing-by and ready to take off at his call. But he'd been informed by Oberkommando Wehrmacht that the Luftwaffe 'wasn't available for road convoy protection', when he'd suggested that air-coverage should be provided over his panzergrenadier regiments. Even his priceless Mk VI Tigers and Mk V Panthers had had to make out with Fieseler Fi 156s. Lutz would have to rely upon the SdKfz 10/4 half-tracks!

So, the column began to thread its way westwards towards the Arlanc junction with the main D906 road and the D202, to proceed north when all civilian traffic had been cleared from the highway beyond the Cleremont-Ferrand crossroads. This was a security measure, as well as helping the vehicles maintain an operational speed. Even so, with the column stretching over thirteen kilometres, there were still units at the St Etienne laager a couple of hours after the leading elements had covered half the distance to their overnight rendezvous in the Fôret d'Ivers, three kilometres south-west of the town of Vichy.

At the point, scout car commanders spared neither time nor effort in making sure the road ahead lay clear. Whenever the maps indicated a spread of dead ground, they trundled across country with the schutzpanzerwagens on their tails, roaring into the hollows at full throttle with hands on smoke plungers on the chance of running headlong into a Maquis ambush. But they found nothing. Each and every hollow was deserted, with only the summer breeze stirring the cornflowers and poppies across the vast stretches of meadow and wheatland.

But, as more time passed, a nagging worry began to replace their initial relief. They knew what had happened in Talmont-les-deux-Ponts, for officers and men of the 2nd Company had been quick to boast of their rape of the village. And raped it they had, by Christ! So where were the French? It wasn't likely they'd take that lying down!

But still there was nothing! For all the Maquis seemed to care the SS could be sitting in their trucks sipping their looted cognac with their helmets hooked over their equipment and the breeze blowing cool through their hair. Not a single shot! Not a single French child throwing a stone! Not even a Frenchwoman spitting on their vehicle!

So what had the French in mind?

There were certainly plenty of them about. The streets of

towns and villages were lined with civilians standing two and three deep in places. But these were broody people – which told the Germans that news of the reprisals at Talmont-les-deux-Ponts had reached them, too. Yet there were no shouts of hate. No tossing of quicklime and muck in toilet pails into the open wells of the schutzpanzerwagens and flak half-tracks. No amplified 'Marseillaise' blasting from loudspeakers.

These were also silent people. People whose hate burned deep in their eyes, the hard set of their jaws and in the pallor of their cheeks.

So what did they have planned for the Uber Alles Waffen SS Panzergrenadiers?

Obersturmbannfuhrer Otto Lutz, who observed what was going on around him with a studied frown, knew they were heading for some kind of a showdown. But what? Had it not been for the incident at Talmont he might have taken a crowd of civilian hostages and stuck them out in front of the convoy in an open truck. Women and children, primarily! Made the buggers uncomfortable and promised them instant death by flame gun if any Frenchman made a wrong move along the route! That would have dampened the Resistance! Seeing the women and children drenched in burning napalm! But now he daren't! Not after Talmont. He'd have to try and play it as canny as the French.

At seven pm there came a signal from the rear of the column to the effect that the last vehicles of the convoy were just leaving the St Etienne laager. That caused Lutz more worries. He immediately summoned an 'O' Group for all officers above hauptsturmfuhrer and found they had fears running parallel to his own. Could be that the Maquis were planning to maul the rear of the column. They'd done that before. He sent a signal back for them to thicken the armoured screen at the rear and include flame-throwing panzers. Then he dismissed the 'O' Group and the officers returned to their stations along the convoy with their minds none the less fraught.

Two hours later the first echelon of armoured cars turned from the D906 road on to a graded earth track which led into the Fôret d'Ivres.

The information was radioed back down the column to Otto Lutz and he breathed a heavy sigh of relief. This meant that his forward elements were firmly anchored and the rest were closing and reducing their vulnerability with every turn of their wheels. Tomorrow, they'd be in the Occupied Zone and most of their apprehensions would have evaporated, leaving them with little more than a mad dash to Argentan and a link with the rest of the division. He radioed back for them to step up speed. Shorten distances between vehicles. A few busted wings were preferable to being caught on the road in failing light. Put a jerk into it! There'd be a hot meal and rum for every man in the laager tonight.

And so there was.

By ten, the last of the rearguard armoured cars was churning along the now deeply rutted tracks which weaved into the depths of the Fôret d'Ivers. There, the trees were old and reaching to heights of thirty metres and more. This was an ideal spot for a divisional laager, for the branches of these mighty trees converged over the tracks and there were enough natural clearings to harbour all the vehicles without having to bulldoze more at the last minute.

The military police were in good humour as they marshalled the last echelons to pre-allocated sites, where the men climbed down stiffly to stretch their legs on earth thick with a century's leaf mould and strewn with pine cones. They slid their heavy equipment from their shoulders and paraded by platoons to collect dixies of hot stew which the cooks had prepared in rapid time from dehydrated composite rations, supplemented by looted game and poultry. Afterwards came hot chocolate generously laced with rum and with hard-tack biscuits to nibble – a traditional treat for supermen of the SS. Traditional but less frequent! Yet, all the more to be appreciated after a day when they'd expected trouble and had made their bound without a single casualty. It appeared that the French had got the message at last. Talmont had done the trick! Old von Sahlenburg at St Etienne had known all along what he was about. Oberkommando Wehrmacht should have listened to him earlier – and they would have if Keitel hadn't got the shits!

So, those grenadiers not detailed for guard duty sprawled in platoon groups on the soft earth, smoking, sipping their hot chocolate and rum, all of them animated at the prospect of what the next few days were likely to bring. They'd heard they'd be pitched on the hinge of the Allied bridgehead, between the American and the Canadian armies. Easy Fox! That was their codename for it! What a hell of a time they were going to have! They'd chase the bloody Yanks straight back into the sea. Rommel and his Panzer Group B would see to that! Already the British were pinned down fast at Caen. And rumours that the American 3rd Army was preparing to loop south-west towards Falaise was all so much balls. General Patton? Who, for Christ's sake, was General Patton? It was a safe bet that Rommel didn't know either. But Patton would know soon enough when the Desert Fox got round to him and he saw the Tigers and the Panthers of the Uber Alles Waffen SS Division brewing up his tin-plate Shermans!

Most of the grenadiers heard the distant throb of aero engines minutes before the air-sentries began cranking their sirens. Even then, their efforts were far from co-ordinated and the troops sleeping beneath the trees did little more than stir in their blankets with half an eye open to the sky. There was no air-raid drill, anyway. Neither had slit-trenches been dug, for it was considered that the chance of an air-raid on what was a secret rendezvous was so remote that it would be a waste of effort for men, wearied after a full day's convoy duty, to hack out century-old tree roots. Each platoon had, therefore, provided its own sentries and that was considered adequate.

As the sirens persisted and the drum-drum of aircraft increased to a roar, many of the grenadiers got sleepily to their feet to move into the nearest clearing open to the sky. This was more out of interest than precautionary. Were these enemy aircraft? Or were they Luftwaffe forming up in strength to hit the Allied beachheads? Luftwaffe, please God! Air support was all the panzer regiments needed to clinch the battle of Normandy. Luftwaffe, please God!

But when they orientated the flight path of these aircraft they saw they were approaching from the north-west — not from the south! They were high, too. Bloody high! Maybe six-thousand metres. Like formations of silver pencils with the moon glistening off their bright fuselages. They could only be American. Yanks! Probably heading for the Wehrmacht concentrations around Lyon. Or railheads? Road communication centres? Radar installations? Shipping on the Rhone? They'd be planning to knock hell out of Lyon! Virtually undefended. Hitting Oberkommando below the belt!

In the Fôret d'Ivres the officers stood with their men, eyes fixed on the velvet summer sky and the moving pattern of giant aircraft. Now they could identify them: United States Army

Air Corps B-29 'Flying Fortresses'. Hundreds of the bastards! All flying on the same course as though deployed for high-level precision attack.

Christ! But Lyon and maybe St Etienne, too, was going to catch a packet from this lot!

It was at that point in time that Obersturmbannfuhrer Otto Lutz and his second-in-command, Obersturmbannfuhrer Karl Maltzen, OC the 2nd Panzergrenadier Regiment Bormann, decided to take a look.

Lutz got up irritably from a table in the operation commander's tent, which had been erected in an isolated clearing where two staff cars were also parked and with a section of panzergrenadiers on guard duty. Otto Lutz was taking no chances as far as his personal safety was concerned!

They had dined well – so far! The paté-de-fois-gras had been as delicate as the Château de la Tour, and there was every indication that the woodcock would be just as pleasantly piquant. And now there were some bloody Yank aircraft buzzing about overhead and making hell of the meal. As he left the tent he snatched the napkin from his belt and tossed it angrily on to the table, immediately rounding on the first sentry he came upon, glaring into the man's startled face.

'What the hell's going on?' he demanded to know and the grenadier stumbled hurriedly through his present-arms drill and swallowed in a dry throat before attempting to reply. He'd never met an obersturmbannfuhrer face to face before. He pointed upwards at the formation of bombers now coming directly overhead.

'Americans, sir!'

He'd heard snatches of conversation from the anti-aircraft and flak details.

'Probably on their way to Lyon!'

'Ah!' Lutz turned to Maltzen and shrugged. Wake the desk-bound idle devils up in Lyon and that couldn't be all bad! Anyway, it was nothing to do with the Uber Alles Division, was it?

Maltzen also shrugged and they turned back into the tent where they hadn't even bothered to douse the light. Damned woodcock would be ruined if they hung about outside much longer.

It was then that the sentry suddenly forgot he was a mere SS-mann and yelled shrilly at the officers.

'Christ! But they're bombing! Look!' Then he remembered himself and sprang to attention, his rifle butt slamming into the ground by his right toe. 'I mean, look, sir! You can see the bombs!'

Lutz and Maltzen spun round together. This man was a bloody fool! What was he talking about? There wasn't an officer below the rank of battalion commander in the 32nd Waffen SS Uber Alles Division who'd known of this secret location in the Fôret d'Ivres. How could they be bombing? He continued to stare angrily into the sky. They'd be dropping tinfoil strips to fox the Lyon radar tracking their flight path. Bombing? Bloody ridiculous!

'They are bombs, Otto.'

Maltzen breathed the words and, as he did so, the anti-aircraft sirens took up the warning and as the men cranked desperately on the handles, the forest rang with their banshee shrieking.

But the grenadiers already knew there was little they could do about the American B-29s. These giant bombers, flying at an altitude of 6,000 metres, couldn't be reached by any of the division's flak-guns. They were equipped for fighter-bombing strafing and some harrying of short take-off aircraft, but not for bombers at such a ceiling.

The first sticks released simultaneously from the leading squadron had flares dispersed amongst them, bursting open as they fell much slower than the bombs on their tiny parachutes, turning night into day above the Fôret d'Ivres. Suddenly there were shadows everywhere and the SS men leapt to their weapons with the magnesium light glinting from their helmets and heightening the pallor of their faces.

'Scatter! Scatter!'

The NCOs were quick to react to a threat they had never anticipated. No slit-trenches! No cover anywhere in this bloody wood! Not even an irrigation ditch! The best they could do was lie up against a tree and pray to God they'd find the trunk between them and the bomb.

'Scatter! Scatter! Scatter!'

Veterans of the Russian campaign panicked with the service men. It was easier to be brave facing a living enemy—but when the enemy was six thousand metres high and doing nothing more than squinting down a bomb-sight there was no call for personal courage.

The flares thickened. The second squadron was hanging course for its first bombing run, even before the first sticks had landed.

'Christ! Christ Almighty!'

Lutz and Maltzen remained where they were standing, outwardly calm and relaxed, watching the reaction of the grenadiers who'd been ordered to scatter, gratified to see their junior officers strolling apparently unconcernedly through the trees, setting an example to their commands.

That was how an officer should behave. Self-discipline was a priority, even in a dicey situation such as this, Lutz remarked.

Anyway, the first stick of bombs was going to miss the laager area by kilometres. He could already see them slanting away to the east. Daylight precision bombing? Maybe! But certainly not night-precision bombing! His lips curled as he turned back to Maltzen. Bloody Yanks! As green in the air as they were in battle. They'd make the bastards pay for tonight once the division got itself operational in Normandy!

But Maltzen was shaking his head.

'These are only the pathfinders, Otto,' he said patiently in his customary quiet tones. 'The main force will home in on the flares. Particularly once the woods get alight.'

Lutz breathed a great sigh. Yes! Maltzen had a point there. Besides, there were so many of the bastards they couldn't all miss their targets. That had also been a decisive element in the battles in Normandy centred round the Utah and Omaha beaches. The Americans had had so much bloody equipment and they hadn't minded losing it. They just went on piling in all the time. Using a coal hammer to squash a spider . . . squash a spider?

CRASH!

The first stick of bombs exploded roughly where Lutz had anticipated it would, in open meadowland some two kilometres to the east. There followed a roaring series of flashes, seemingly all in line, the sky above them momentarily a searing vermilion which died as suddenly as it had erupted.

Any moment now there'd be more explosions and probably right where they were standing.

A sudden fury, born of his impotence, hit Lutz and he crashed the ball of his right fist into the open palm of his other hand. Where was the bloody Luftwaffe? Where were Junkers-187 night-fighters which were supposed to have wreaked such carnage on the invasion beaches? Hadn't even the radar picked this lot up, yet, for Christ's sake?

CRASH!

The second stick exploded much closer and the sudden change in air pressure caused the tent to billow, dragging on the guy ropes.

Lutz shook his head bitterly. Maybe, after all, he was to die in this forest in the heart of enemy France. And one that wasn't even marked on his operations map!

'How'd the Yanks know about this laager, Karl?' he asked presently in much quieter tones.

Maltzen shrugged.

'I suppose the Resistance. Either directly or indirectly.'

Lutz pondered on that for a few seconds, then nodded thoughtfully.

'It has to be, hasn't it?' he agreed. 'The bloody French! But how, for Christ's sake, did they find out? Surely to God we don't have an informer on our Staff, do we Karl?'

Maltzen smiled wanly as he shook his head. There could be no informer in an SS division and that was for sure.

CRASH!

The two regimental commanders were buffeted by the blast. Bombs were falling closer, but none yet appeared to have landed within the perimeter of the laager area. There'd been no frantic shrieks of agony; no cries for stretcher-bearers. But the explosions were getting close! The sky was swarming with aircraft which would have been sitting ducks for Junkers Ju-187s, Maltzen reflected . . . sitting ducks! They were even taking their time, the squadrons banking in wide circles as soon as they'd let their first sticks go, pinpointing their targets for the second runs. More incendiary bombs were thickening up the high explosive and the squadron which had just bracketed the edge of the forest had released further flares.

CRASH!

Sudden shrieks of pain cascaded from somewhere amongst the trees. Frenzied screams from a troop of grenadiers manning the inadequate flak half-tracks. Almost immediately followed the sound of automobile engines being jerked into life. Ambulances came racing through the trees heading for where the screams were loudest.

Blood to the Yanks!

They'd sit up there and take their time because the bastards knew they were safe! They could wipe out a couple of regiments of grenadiers without having to take a bullet in return. Jesus! But how the French would be enjoying this!

With Commanders Gunter Haller and Horst Kaser still unaccounted for, Untersturmfuhrer Werner Odermatt was holding on to his control of Number 2 Panzergrenadier Company. He had been proud of his temporary appointment, particularly during the early part of the day when he'd looked down the battalion column of route and seen it tag on to the mighty regimental convoy.

That had been good! Probably one of the highlights of his life.

He'd wished his brother, Franz, who'd served with the Grossdeutschland Division in Russia and had somehow managed to get back home with a broken spine, had seen him today. Now, Franz spent most of his time in bed under his parents' care, but his interest was still centred on the Panzer SS battalions and he lived for the letters which Werner wrote him from the Uber Alles.

Yes, Odermatt had thought that morning, he'd have given a lot for Franz to have seen him at the head of Number 2 Company column!

It was an invincible force which had moved north through France – even without the Mk V Panthers and the Mk VI Tiger battalions. More than enough to persuade the snivelling French peasants who was boss! Second-class citizens the lot of 'em, with their stinking pig farms littering the countryside, their half-dozen cattle doddering about under the trees and their tumbledown villages not fit for clean-minded people to live in! No wonder the miserable sods were quiet! They could, at least, recognise a superior race when they saw one. Now he knew how brother Franz had felt when he'd roared across the Russian steppes in his armoured car at the head of Grossdeutschland!

Odermatt's cup of happiness had been overflowing when he'd been summoned personally to report to Regimental Commander Obersturmbannfuhrer Otto Lutz. He had slammed to attention before the great man and in crisp tones proclaimed that Number 2 Company was secure in laager. No casualties had been sustained during the journey. Guards and sentries had been mounted within the company area! Sir!

That had been three hours ago.

Three hours? Was that all?

Now Odermatt was standing with Untersturmfuhrer Wolfgang Sieloff, Number Two Platoon Commander, and at twenty-one a year younger than Odermatt. They had anxious eyes on the sky in much the same way as Lutz had stood with Maltzen minutes earlier.

'Bastards!'

Sieloff turned to grin at Odermatt's sudden eruption. He was a tall, rangy, young man with close-cropped fair hair who had been an economics student at Bielefeld University. He'd always believed that the war would be over before he got his call-up papers, but he'd been proved wrong. The Waffen SS had insisted on his recruitment to officer rank because of his physique and, also, because of his education. But Hauptsturmfuhrer Horst Kaser had always claimed that the boy's pure Aryan appearance had clinched him for the Uber Alles. Yet, sadly, Sieloff hadn't matured into an outstanding officer.

Odermatt, a smaller, dark-haired, intense, young man held a similar personal impression. He rounded on him angrily at the reaction.

'What the hell is there to laugh at?'

Sieloff continued to smile.

'There's not a thing we can do about these Yanks, Werner,' he remarked laconically. 'We might just as well lie down in the trees!'

As he spoke, a stick of bombs which had been in their vision within seconds of leaving the now-banking aircraft, slanted towards them. The officers ducked on reflex as the long black cylinders, appearing to be little over tree top height, passed overhead. They threw themselves to the ground amidst a running chain of mighty, ear-splitting explosions which made it sound as though the universe was disintegrating around them.

They shoved their faces deeper into the earth as blast whipped foliage from the trees and heavy branches began to fall about them in a kind of slow motion as gyrating air currents still supported them. From the area where the bombs had landed there came the harsh rasping sound of splintering wood and tall trees snapped off at their roots, bringing down smaller trees with them.

Unaccountably there followed a silence. An eerie, forboding silence which chilled the men where they lay. It was a silence which seemed to persist interminably and one from which even the rumble of the B-29s had vanished.

The two officers raised their heads, looking questioningly at each other when all hell broke loose around them. And it was at that moment that Untersturmfuhrers Odermatt and Sieloff knew that for them the war had started.

Afterwards, neither could clearly recall the sequence of events which followed during the next half-hour in the Fôret d'Ivres. Like most of the SS officers they'd acted on their own initiative, dispersing grenadiers and their vehicles, sending them scooting through the trees, seeking open clearings. Casualties followed such reckless driving. Men were run down and there were branches of trees low enough to break the teeth and gouge out the eyes of drivers who relied too much on the light from American flares, burning vehicles and undergrowth. In the chaos, men stumbled over their wounded comrades, slipping on slimy pools of blood and entrails, callously ignoring screams for help because there was nothing they could do: anyway, they were being rounded up by their officers who yelled for them to disperse to survive. And they meant the division – not the grenadiers!

Trucks and half-tracks caught fire, littering the woodland tracks, and the American bomb-aimers recognised these for what they were and delayed their releases to home in on such welcome markers.

Five kilometres north at Oberkommando Wehrmacht Regional HQ, Vichy, Regional Commander Obersturmbannfuhrer Walter Emmerling stared in horror from the window of his top floor apartment in the Hotel de la Paix as the American B-29 bombers began their first runs.

It was as apparent to him as it was to his Staff that the two panzergrenadier regiments in the Fôret d'Ivres were in for a thrashing and there was nothing he, nor they, could do about it. In the planning they'd banked on no Allied air interference. How could there be? The laager location was classified top secret!

So, as the bombardment stepped up its fury, Emmerling did all that was left to him. He despatched an aide to L'Hôpital Vichy and had them prepare as many wards as they could to accommodate panzergrenadier wounded. He also sent a despatch rider to the Fôret d'Ivres where the man bravely struggled to give Obersturmbannfuhrer Otto Lutz a personal message to tell him that such arrangements had been laid on.

Lutz was quick to react, immediately appreciative that other people had acknowledged the regiments' predicament and he had ambulances loaded with batches of the more seriously wounded.

But before they could leave the forest, the French, anticipating help from Vichy, dynamited the two main bridges over the Dore river. If the Boches needed to get their wounded to hospital, then from now on they'd have to make themselves a ferry!

Within half an hour, the last of the B-29s had turned for home and, had a bomber of such a size been capable of executing a victory roll, then no doubt most of them would have done so. There had been an undeniable exhilaration in the way they had lifted their heavy noses as they trundled back north, seeking altitude above the German flak and the night-fighters which radar would have in store for them somewhere en route. But to the officers and men of the panzergrenadier regiments, bleeding and disillusioned in the blazing forest, it was apparent that the Americans had completed their bombing programme without sustaining a single casualty over the target area. Out of a hundred and more, not one bloody bomber had fallen! Not one!

Now they were already reorganising themselves into something like an SS force again, leaving vehicles to burn themselves out and doing no more than contain fires in surrounding undergrowth which could hinder their work.

Lutz sent a detachment of engineers to repair the east bridge over the Dore, giving it priority. His plan was to shift the main force from the Fôret d'Ivres at dawn. He would leave a token rear party to see the wounded to hospital and patch up any damaged vehicles which could be made sufficiently mobile to complete the journey north. From now on, the convoy would have to be in two echelons. Meanwhile, he'd leave Maltzen in command and take a staff car direct to Rommel's Headquarters at Army Group B. There'd be a hell of a row awaiting him and, God knows, he'd more than likely lose his command.

Untersturmfuhrer Werner Odermatt took a parade-state as soon as the confusion in the wood eased. Hauptscharfuhrer Walter Muller reported a total of eighty-six fit men in Number 2 Company who'd survived the bombs. The information caused Odermatt to breathe a sigh of relief. Twenty-five casualties from a near-establishment strength was bad enough, but, God, it could have been a bloody sight worse!

He detailed his platoon commanders to continue sorting out the chaos within the company lines and to report to him how many of the twenty-five were dead and how many were seriously wounded. Thank Christ all the officers and most of the NCOs had managed to survive!

It was as the new dawn stole coldly across the pulverised forest that Odermatt began to appreciate just how lucky Number 2 Company had been. The scene before him reminded him of the illustrations of no-man's-land he'd seen in training manuals which had been published during the 1914—18 war when his father and three uncles had fought against these same enemies.

He left his company lines where grenadiers were searching round for equipment lost during the bombardment; servicing MG-42 machine guns; 8cm Granatwerfer mortars; panzerfausts and panzerschrecks; their G-41 (M) rifles and MP-40 Schmeiser machine pistols. Riflemen were also cleaning machine-gun belts, taking out each round, laboriously polishing and smearing it with oil, as well as the loop in the belt, before re-inserting it.

The activity reassured Odermatt. It demonstrated the strength and resilience of an SS unit. These men had survived what could well be their heaviest bombardment of the war and, already, they were shrugging it off, anxious to get to the Normandy battlefront. What they'd experienced last night would fan the hate they'd need when they came face-to-face with Yank infantry.

But as he moved through the forest some of his composure began to ebb. He came upon a pioneer detail, the men balanced precariously on makeshift ladders constructed from fallen branches, prodding with sticks at what at first glance looked like bundles of rags wedged amongst the high branches.

Odermatt halted, interested, but when some of these bundles came tumbling down he saw that the rags were brown-stained fragments of field uniform and the heavy objects inside them were human limbs. Despite himself his face blanched and when one of the bundles fell at his feet he strode quickly away from it. Only when he noticed one of the pioneer NCOs watching him did he turn to look back. It was a part of an arm severed from the middle of the forearm to the shoulderblade, the bone grey-white against the blood-coagulated flesh which fringed it.

A head dropped close by with a bulged helmet still strapped incongruously about the chin. The eyes had gone and so had the top jaw, whilst stubs of broken teeth protruded from the lower jaw, clamping on to what remained of the nose. The hair which spread from beneath the rim of the helmet was as Aryan blond as Sieloff's.

Farther along Odermatt spotted a line of bomb craters and took the chance to escape from the pioneer NCO's condemning stare. He saw then that some of the holes had been used to dump more severed limbs, as well as shattered bodies which must have been at the centre of the explosion.

He strode deeper into the forest where rutted tracks indicated where some of the vehicles and half-tracks had made a final frantic attempt to escape the full force of the bombardment. Here, as he hurried on, he found his bitterness and resentment beginning to boil inside him.

Christ! But somebody would have to pay for this! Somebody would! Either the Yanks or the bastard French Maquis. The French! It was they who'd given the location to the Americans. Somehow they'd traced the laager. And they'd be made to pay a dozen times for each and every SS-mann who'd died in this bloody forest! The lot of the bastards! Men, women and children! No quarter! He'd see to it himself that what had happened at Talmont-les-deux-Ponts would look like a picnic in comparison!

He halted abruptly, staring ahead to where the trees arched over what, at one time or another, might have been a firebreak. There, half-hidden in the ditch, he spotted a schutzpanzerwagen on its side. Both its tracks were missing and most of the superstructure had disintegrated. Then, farther along, was a second, still smouldering and farther still, a third. Odermatt increased his pace, planning to take a look at the damage and see if there were any wounded still lying there. But as he got closer he found that the dark stain he'd noticed smeared across the front of the first half-track was all that was left of the SS driver who'd been squashed like a fly against a wall. His blood and sinew had coagulated in the heat from the exploded fuel tank, leaving all that remained of the empty shell of the body stuck to the armour.

He turned around to head back to his company lines. This kind of reconnaissance was doing him no good at all. He was as sickened by what he had seen as he was by the knowledge that, had there been no bombardment, the column would already have been heading north. Now it was becoming questionable whether the Panzergrenadier Regiments Hess and Bormann would be able to join Rommel's Army Group B for some time.

But, as he'd already vowed, he'd make sure somebody paid.

A personal vendetta against the French?

That was a promise! On his brother's name!

Unteroffizier Fritz Allemann was forty-six and a platoon sergeant with Number 3 Company of the 603rd Infantry Battalion. He had been present during the abortive attempt at the liberation of Oberstleutnant Overath's force from the Maquis at Talmont-les-deux-Ponts, but had not taken an active part. His platoon had been positioned as flank guard to Major Emmerich's headquarters on the Loze river and had not even been called upon to put down supporting fire. When the Oberstleutnant had come forward to offer a truce, Allemann had been as relieved as Emmerich.

As with most of the survivors of that action, Allemann was trying to live down the ignominy of defeat. Oberkommando Wehrmacht's regional office had reacted by shifting the battalion out of the Chateau d'Aubigny into requisitioned civilian billets within the city perimeter of St Etienne. There, they had been told, General Friedel von Sahlenburg intended to keep a personal eye on them.

A personal eye!

There wasn't a man in the 603rd who hadn't heard of von Sahlenburg's ruthless impatience, nor of his ambitions. The fact that both Overath and Emmerich had disappeared from the battalion scene gave credence to the general's rumoured terrorist campaign currently being planned against the civilian population. Most of the men of the 603rd shied at the prospect of being used as SS or, worse, Gestapo; but there was nothing they could do about it unless they were prepared to risk being sacrificed to the Maquis guns when the next action erupted.

So, at a little after 5 am on the morning following the American bombing of the 2nd and 3rd Panzergrenadier Regiments, Unteroffizier Fritz Allemann trudged behind the forward rifle section leading his little band of Platoon Headquarters. The other two sections followed at ten metre intervals. Neither he, nor they, nor the officer who'd briefed them for this daily routine patrol, knew anything of the disaster which had befallen the panzergrenadiers during the hours of darkness. They had heard the distant rumble of massed bombers and the subsequent half-hour's pandemonium, but none had connected the air-raid with the Uber Alles Division. At the first flurry of explosions they had crowded the windows of their billets and watched the steady glow of fire creep across the distant horizon. Some had been interested enough to produce field compasses, range-finders and maps with which they had plotted the target area to be the communications centre of Vichy. Accurate, but not accurate enough!

This was a dull, clammy morning which contrasted sharply with the bright sunshine of the past few days. A pale mist hung over the Loire which, at that time of early morning, looked not unlike a November fog.

The leading section headed directly for the river, their eyes still heavy with sleep as they followed the mechanical movements of the men marching a few metres ahead. These routine patrols were a bore and a bloody waste of time – what, in battle, would have amounted to a dawn stand-to. But here there was no enemy facing them from parallel lines of slit-trenches, no high-explosive shells bouncing down on them to herald a new day. Here, there was only the bloody, goddamn French Resistance who could be doing something or nothing at all. Usually nothing, so close to St Etienne! Now and then they might come across a few teller mines buried a couple of centimetres beneath the road surface at a place where the first of the staff cars was likely to pass. Bastards! They were too bloody efficient at pasting over the holes they cut in the tarmac, which meant that so far as the battalion's self-respect went, the 603rd had nothing to gain and everything to lose. There was also occasional other Maquis activity. Things like busted sluice gates, sunken barges, blocked drain channels – all of them carefully selected and sabotaged so that the Wehrmacht patrols could get themselves a hell of a lot of problems before they were even spotted!

The platoon approached the river across an expanse of meadow and scrappy woodland. The landscape improved with the brightening dawn, but on the other side of the river was an industrial estate which appeared to specialise in fabrication work. The giant hammers were already beginning to pound and the hiss of the steam valves on the presses reached the

Germans as they moved down to the water's edge, where they shambled to a halt and stared across.

'Come on you shower! Wake up, for Christ's sake! Let's put some bloody life into it!'

Allemann rounded on the two rear sections where some of the men had dropped on to their haunches and begun tossing pebbles into the oily current. He had fought in the 1940 blitzkrieg which had decimated the French and Belgian armies and sent the British Expeditionary Force scooting back across the Channel from Dunkirk. Churchill had proclaimed that a British victory at the time. The Wehrmacht had pissed themselves at that! But a few days later an RAF Spitfire had hurtled from a low cloud ceiling and blasted him and his rifle section with cannon shells. Now, he was back on active service again after four endless years and most of that time in a military hospital. He still had a limp and he still remembered those early days of the war when the invincible Wehrmacht had hunted a tin-pot enemy who'd called themselves soldiers! Maybe, right now, the 603rd was every bit as much a bloody rabble, but one thing was for certain: his platoon were going to be soldiers if it took him the rest of his life to do it!

'Move yourselves you idle buggers!' He bawled angrily at Paul Schindleholz, commanding the point section. 'Gefreiter! Take upstream!' Then, to Hans Dienst commanding the rearguard. 'You take downstream! The rest come inland with me as far as the sluices. Yell, if any of you find anything. Now go to it!'

He paused, scowling after them as they moved off in the directions he had indicated. After they had covered a good fifty metres he led the remainder north towards the sluice gates, unguarded and still operated by French civilian labour. Hell of a risk!

The day brightened further as the platoon rummaged along the riverbank in accord with their standard brief. It was a desultory kind of a search, but even Allemann had to admit that a man couldn't maintain a soldier-like bearing when he was rooting through old packing cases and industrial rubbish.

'Unteroffizier!'

Allemann jerked up sharply at the sharp cry from downstream.

'What is it?'

Gefreiter Hannans Dienst was standing on top of the

riverbank, his Schmeiser machine pistol held above his head signalling. He was about a hundred and fifty metres away. The rest of the section was crowded at the water's edge.

'We've got something here, Unteroffizier! Bodies!'

Allemann would have liked to have demanded what bodies and how many, but he didn't. This wasn't the kind of thing which occupying troops should shout about along a deserted stretch of river.

'Be with you Dienst! Stay there!'

He left the other section upstream and hurried the remainder of the platoon to join Dienst's section.

There were two bodies lying in a few centimetres of water, stirring restlessly in a long narrow pool separated from the main river flow by shallow grey sandbanks.

They were civilians, dressed almost identically in black suits, white shirts, black ties. They were both hatless. The shorter of the two men appeared to be unmarked. His face was almost serene in death as though, at the last minute before his execution, he'd been spared some horror which he had expected to be his. This probability was given credence by the condition of his companion. He was a taller man, heavier built though of about the same age, but the snarl on the dead face contorted and twisted in a final agony, told its own story. The skull had been splintered into the brain by what appeared to have been one of the Gestapo's favourite make-you-talk devices. The head-crusher! Across the man's forehead were two deep, black weals where the steel bands had bitten hard into the flesh and there was a jagged hole at the back of the head where the screwed plate had driven through into the brain. There was little doubt that this unfortunate man would have told his tormentors all they'd wanted to know, for few men could survive a head-crusher expertly applied. Each gentle turn of the crank usually had them screaming for death within the hour.

Allemann looked down from the top of the bank to where Dienst was bending over the bodies.

'Jews?' Allemann asked.

Dienst nodded. 'Looks like it, Unteroffizier! Gestapo's been at 'em!'

'Do they have papers?'

'I've not looked. Thought I'd better wait for you.'

Allemann scrambled awkwardly down the loose bank
90

dragging his right leg, but making little of the pain. He stared contemplatively at the bodies in much the same way as the gefreiter had done.

They were Jews all right! He wondered what the poor bastards had done or what they'd known to make the Gestapo put the screws on them. Then he stooped to run his hands expertly through their sodden clothes, stirring gobs of coagulated black blood from the man's crushed head. From each of the inner jacket pockets he took the usual kind of cellophane wrapper containing Carte d'Identite, Permit de Conduire and civilian ration card. Then he scowled from one to the other, attempting to correlate the photographs on the identity cards with the dead faces.

'Jews!' he confirmed more to himself than to anyone else, reading out the names. 'Jean Leveque! Israel Latouche! So!'

'Israel?' Dienst echoed the name and Allemann looked up to shrug.

'That's right! The poor bastard with his head caved in. That was Israel Latouche.'

'What happens now, Unteroffizier?'

Allemann glared at him.

'What the hell do you think happens? That we carry the buggers home?' His voice curdled in sarcasm and he turned away from the section leader to a signaller who was sitting on the bank, adjusting the dials of a field R/T set. 'Branck! Tell Sunray we've got a coupla Jew corpses who look as though they've had a rough time. Tell 'em I say the Gestapo shouldn't be so bloody untidy. Tell 'em to tell the Gestapo to come an' collect their own litter. We're supposed to be a military reconnaissance patrol, not bloody morticians!'

It was the best part of an hour before the St Etienne Gestapo Chief, Oberscharfuhrer Franz Leimgruber, arrived on the scene in the usual Gestapo-type black saloon car and wearing the usual Gestapo-type black trilby and belted mackintosh. He found Allemann and his patrol making sure the bodies didn't go floating down the Loire, in a bid to prevent other French Jews from appearing on the scene and seeing what had happened to two of their faith.

But when Oberscharfuhrer Leimgruber saw the corpses the breeziness suddenly left him. His face paled visibly — which caused Allemann to smile, for he'd have thought that a Gestapo chief, of all people, wouldn't have been upset at the sight of the end result of a head-crushing party.

But less than twelve hours earlier Leimgruber had seen things which Allemann had not seen — ID photographs of two missing officers of the 32nd Panzer Division Waffen SS Grenadier Regiments: Sturmbannfuhrer Gunter Haller and Hauptsturmfuhrer Horst Kaser. Now, here they were, both of them dressed up in Jewish clothes, carrying Jewish papers and floating dead in the Loire.

Maquis!

He smiled sardonically to himself. Here was a savage and ironic twist if ever there was one — senior SS officers rigged up as Jews and tossed in the river like so much offal. It was a stroke of inventive genius of which the Gestapo, itself, might have been proud.

As for Haller with his skull caved in, SS Panzergrenadier battalion commander or not, he'd have talked! Despite his distinguished service he was flesh and blood like any other officer. Poor bastard! That this should happen to a soldier like Haller. A *Ritter Kreuz* was no match for a head-crusher! For both Germans and French would soon know who'd given the Fôret d'Ivres laager location to the Americans. As intermediaries the Maquis had wasted no time!

He glared up angrily at Allemann who was sitting on the bank, no longer interested now that the Gestapo was on hand.

'Who knows about these?' Leimgruber snarled, at which Allemann immediately bridled, resenting the tone.

'The men you see here! We're a platoon, not a bloody company!'

Leimgruber ignored that.

'Come down here, Unteroffizier!'

Again, Allemann descended the bank, again having trouble with his malformed leg.

'What is it?'

Leimgruber pointed at the corpses.

'Tell your men to keep their mouths shut about these,' he said. 'No explanations! Just keep their mouths shut! If any of them talks they'll have to answer personally to the Gestapo. Understand?'

Chapter Four

Less than forty years ago the lovely village of St-Honor-sur-Clair had a legend all of its own.

This legend claimed that when the angels came to earth seeking a second paradise they happened upon the sweet-scented hills surrounding the beautiful Clair valley. There they paused, gazing over the sun-drenched slopes where happy people worked their fruitful vineyards. These were young and industrious people, sun tanned to the hi on the tawny earth, and their contentment with the life with which *le bon Dieu* had blessed them was there for all to see.

Surely, the angels said, if ever there was a heaven upon earth then this must be it, and they named the tiny settlement above the wide bend in the Clair river after the archangel they revered most of all and whom had blessed them in their search.

They named it: St-Honor!

Over the centuries the village hardly changed. Perhaps the vegetation grew a little greener, the sky became a little bluer, or the colours of the flowers became a little more resplendent. The vines continued to produce a richly red and full-bodied wine and the cattle which grazed in open meadows beyond the hills gave their creamy milk in abundance.

Visitors came from the ends of the earth to wonder and revel in the natural beauty that was St-Honor's. They brought with them ageing aunts for a glimpse of this heaven on earth before the old ladies passed on into the next. They brought cameras, paints, easels, potter's clay and fishing rods, but none were allowed to stay more than a few weeks. The family names of St-Honor could be compared with the burghers' rolls of two centuries earlier, and there would be few changes. Only healthy young women were welcomed, for too much inter-breeding wasn't to be encouraged even in paradise; but most of the men, apart from a mere handful with wanderlust, had been happy to remain to work the land they loved.

And so the years had passed as placidly and elegantly as the gurgling Clair until, one day during the late summer of 1944,

St-Honor suddenly shrivelled and perished. Within hours on that terrible day the beauty, the tranquillity and the passion which had been hers, was taken away.

Today, not forty years later, there remains but little to be seen of this once heaven on earth. Here and there amongst the now-ravaged vegetation stands a crumbling ruin of ochre-tinted wall, still catching the sun. The smooth green sward of the Champ de Foire is overgrown, pockmarked with clumps of dock and thistle, and the two small hotels which bordered it have long since been bulldozed into the hillside to hide the deepest wounds that were St-Honor's. Even the colour has gone from the hillsides and the Clair river which abounded in life is as dead and dank as a polluted mill stream.

It is as though the angels who found this lovely place have, in their grief and horror at the brutal incomprehensibility of man, taken away the flowers and the wild creatures which swam its river and roamed its woodland.

Why?

Because it was on that late July day in 1944, a warm and balmy summer's afternoon, that the German SS came to St-Honor-sur-Clair.

And when they left, twenty-four hours later, the village was burnt to the ground and the whole population of 568 men, women and children had fallen to their guns and bayonets.

Two hours after Gestapo Chief Oberscharfuhrer Franz Leimgruber had reported the discovery of the dead bodies of Gunter Haller and Horst Kaser in the shallows of the Loire river, Untersturmfuhrer Werner Odermatt was ordered to report to Obersturmbannfuhrer Karl Maltzen who had now taken command of the panzergrenadier convoy north.

Odermatt hurried to his presence with rising apprehension. He could see no reason at all why he'd been singled out from three hundred and more officers in the Fôret d'Ivres laager. He'd taken the Yank bombing with the rest of the troops and he'd since done all he could to get his company sufficiently mobile to join the column with a minimum of delay. So what was eating Maltzen? And, for the matter, where was Lutz? Had Lutz been killed in the bombing, for Christ's sake? He'd have welcomed a speculative word with Sieloff, but avoided him. Seeking Sieloff's reaction would only have lowered his own prestige and probably not helped at all.

When he got to the clearing where the command tent was pitched he at once saw that that part of the forest had escaped bomb blast. The tent wasn't even muddied and the staff car, parked a few metres from it, was undamaged. Evidently, Lutz had already gone ahead in the other staff car — probably to report to General Elsener personally.

He marched briskly up to the open flap of the tent and peered inside. When he noticed Maltzen sitting at a table with a document file spread out in front of him he snapped to attention and saluted.

'Untersturmfuhrer Werner Odermatt reporting! Sir!'

Maltzen scowled irritably at being disturbed. Odermatt bucked at that. Hadn't it been the general who'd sent for him?

Maltzen spoke, giving the platoon commander only half his attention, his eyes still straying over his papers.

'Ah, yes, Odermatt!' The scowl deepened as he looked over the slight figure of the officer now temporarily in command of Number 2 Panzergrenadier Company. 'You've to report to General von Sahlenburg in St. Etienne without delay. Off you go!'

Odermatt hesitated.

'St Etienne, sir?'

Maltzen brought the flat of his hand down hard on the table top.

'You're not deaf are you, Odermatt? You're already aware, I assume, that General von Sahlenburg is OC, OKW, St Etienne region?'

'But of course, sir.'

'Then what the hell are you waiting for, Odermatt? Off you go! Surely as a temporary company commander you've the initiative to organise yourself transport?'

'Sir!'

Odermatt didn't enjoy the journey back along the previous day's convoy route. He put on a private soldier's helmet and greatcoat and took a motorcycle combination with an experienced driver, crouching deep in the sidecar with his eyes on the road ahead and a hand clutching a Luger automatic in the greatcoat pocket. This was bloody dicey and he knew it, but there wasn't a chance in hell of Battalion HQ letting him have a schutzpanzerwagen for such a trip. Temporary company commander or not, he'd have to take a motorcycle combination, and they'd added that the ruling would still have applied even if half the transport hadn't been brewed up during the night!

But as the journey passed he discovered that the French had other things on their minds that day than German motorcyclists. The streets of the towns and villages were even more congested than yesterday, but the attitude of the civilians had changed. Today, these were happy, smiling, French people who crowded the roadside café-bars holding glasses of red wine and singing the Marseillaise. No loudspeakers! Clear, resonant French voices vibrant with patriotism and wine.

Odermatt didn't need telling they were celebrating the American bombing of the Fôret d'Ivres and its quick and ruthless revenge for the SS incident at Talmont-les-deux-Ponts. Once again they'd proved to themselves and to the Wehrmacht that France had found her teeth and that this new eye-for-an-eye policy was on the point of superseding their 'Kill-a-Boche-a-Day!' Soon they'd be openly taking the war to the Wehrmacht.

Odermatt sank deeper into the sidecar, face impassive, avoiding the eyes of the mocking French, but finding some relief in the knowledge that they appeared to be taking a brief respite from their killing, sniping and harassment.

At von Sahlenburg's city-centre HQ he sent the driver to the OR's canteen, dropped the overcoat and helmet into the sidecar, swept on his own peaked service cap and sprinted up the flight of steps at the top of which a couple of sentries sloped arms and saluted.

They directed him to an inner reception office where an unterscharfuhrer directed him to a small office along the corridor. There, a fair-haired hauptsturmfuhrer was sitting not at a desk, but sprawled across a leather armchair turned towards an open window. The officer grinned over his shoulder as Odermatt saluted, pointing to a chair opposite.

'Perhaps you should know that I'm a new boy here, too, Odermatt,' he said conversationally. 'The name's Schroeder. Jurgen Schroeder. I'm one of the general's recent acquisitions, all right?'

Odermatt nodded warily. He'd already noticed the insignia of the Iron Cross, Classes 1 and 2, and it struck him that this young hauptsturmfuhrer could be no ordinary aide. If he were new to St Etienne, then why was he here at all? Surely, such experience would normally have had priority on the Normandy battlefront?

Schroeder took out a slim gold cigarette case from a tunic breast pocket and meticulously lit a cigarette.

'Tell me, Odermatt,' he said in the same quiet tone. 'Were Sturmbannfuhrer Haller and Hauptsturmfuhrer Kaser particularly good friends of yours?'

Odermatt scowled, immediately ill-at-ease, but he managed an indifferent shrug as he held the other's eyes.

'They were my battalion and company commander, sir,' he replied quietly. 'Obviously I had a great deal of personal respect . . .'

'Good! I'm pleased to hear that. Now listen! For I have important news for you.'

And then Schroeder went on to describe in languid, cultured tones how Haller and Kaser had met their deaths. How it was believed that Haller, despite his distinguished service career, had been tortured by the Maquis into giving away the location of the Uber Alles laager in the Fôret d'Ivres. At this point, Schroeder excused Haller in much the same way that Gestapo Chief Leimgruber had classified the sturmbannfuhrer's predicament. He leaned forward, staring into Odermatt's face which had paled to a death-white. Even his lips were bloodless.

'You see, Odermatt, the head-crusher works just as well for the French as it does for our Gestapo. Even so, had Sturmbannfuhrer Haller survived his ordeal he would, without doubt, have been called upon to face a court-martial subsequently, probably an execution squad. One cannot betray a regiment and expect to live, no matter how persistent one's captors. Don't you agree, Odermatt?'

Odermatt nodded weakly, head swimming. He believed that such degradation of a senior SS officer — rigging him up in Jewish clothing, giving him Jewish identity documents and dumping his body on a mudflat alongside a French river — cancelled out his collapse under torture.

'Well, Odermatt? Do you agree or not?'

Odermatt squared his shoulders and met Schroeder's eyes bravely.

'Yes, sir! Of course, I agree!'

'Good! Then we shall now go and see the general together.'

General Friedel von Sahlenburg had not taken the news concerning Haller and Kaser with the equanimity of his two new aides, Bucholz and Schroeder. At the time he had paled to the same shade of white as Odermatt and, momentarily, his head had swum so that he had been compelled to clutch at the corner of his desk for support.

That was a hell of a package for any man to take in one, he told himself: a twenty-five per cent casualty rating amongst men and transport of two panzergrenadier regiments – six battalions! – and then, in the same breath, to learn that the traitor who gave the enemy the location was a life-long friend and holder of the *Ritter Kreuz*!

Unbelievable! Bloody incredible!

Gunter Haller who'd fought the whole way to Dnepropetrovsk and back!

He got up from his chair unsteadily and went over to the drinks cabinet where he poured himself a half-tumbler of neat cognac.

The telephone rang and it was a signal relayed for Obersturmfuhrer Karl Maltzen informing him that Untersturmfuhrer Werner Obermatt, who was temporarily in command of Number 2 Panzergrenadier Company, was on his way to obtain a brief concerning reprisals agaist French civilians.

Reprisals?

Von Sahlenburg clutched the confirmatory message form and stared at it blankly. Reprisals? Who was he supposed to detail? Surely not the 603rd Infantry Battalion! If he'd had Klaus-Dieter Elsener at the other end of the telephone line right now, he'd have made short work of the commander's evasiveness concerning SS reinforcements. Just shows what happens when you take an easy way out with the Maquis. Damn it! Even the bloody 603rd managed to prove that much at Talmont!

When the telephone rang again this was no confirmatory signal, but a personal call from the great man himself, Generalfeldmarschall Walter Keitel, ringing direct from his HQ at Argentan where he'd a man-size battle on his hands.

'Look, Friedel!' Keitel's voice was irritable and it was obvious he was going to be quick to say his piece and ring off. 'I've just heard about the fiasco last night at Vichy and also about Gunter Haller. Elsener's responsibility! Not mine! But you're on the bloody spot and I want to see some positive action taken against these French civilians and without any more delay! Have you got that, Friedel? Right now! You've already had my council order!'

'Yes, sir!' von Sahlenburg replied hurriedly, scared that the Generalfeldmarschal was about to ring off. 'Just one thing, I need troops ...'

'You've got bloody troops! How many more do you want?'

'I've got infantry, but I need SS! I must have SS if we're going to hold the Maquis down.'

'How many SS, for Christ's sake? Don't you realise we need all the SS we can muster here in Normandy ...'

'One company of panzergrenadiers, sir! I could make do with just one company.'

There followed a brief silence during which von Sahlenburg hung on to the phone.

Then Keitel said, 'All right! You've got one company! Make your orders to the 32nd Panzer Division and quote my authority!'

And with that he slammed down the handset, leaving von Sahlenburg staring sightlessly at the wall opposite.

Nevertheless, for all that, he felt a lot easier.

It was a little after 1 am the following morning that Number 2 Panzergrenadier Company stole into the darkened streets of St Etienne in six covered infantry transporters and with a single armoured scout car as escort.

They were hustled into an empty infants' school where blackouts were nailed up at the windows and the first hot meal of the past twenty-four hours was served. For the time being, this SS detachment now under the overall command of OC Oberkommando Wehrmacht, St Etienne Region, had gone to ground.

Von Sahlenburg knew that he had all the time in the world to put Keitel's orders into operation. The longer he took to strike, the better would be his chance of success. Lull the French bastards into a feeling of security. Don't give them a clue there were SS still in the region. Let them believe they'd all gone north to fight the war. That way the Maquis would either continue to lie low or they'd go raise hell some other place in the Zone.

Anyway, he'd made up his mind on one thing! He'd no intention of pitting his SS against armed men, either Maquis or odd bands of guerillas. He'd strike some place where there'd been neither German nor Maquis activity during the whole of the Occupation. Some kilometres from the beaten paths of war and commerce where neither side would normally have anything to gain. Somewhere where life had meandered its way through the war in secure isolation; somewhere where the SS wouldn't be expected and somewhere where they'd find no resistance when they arrived!

This time, he'd show the Wehrmacht how to make reprisals without as much as a single German casualty. It was easy — once they picked the perfect spot to start with and then took it from there!

But where?

Von Sahlenburg didn't know and, at that moment, he didn't care. As he'd said, he had time and he also had a whole Intelligence HQ piled high with large-scale maps of the region.

Later that morning he called in his two aides, Sturm-bannfuhrer Kurt Bucholz and Hauptsturmfuhrer Jurgen Schroeder, to whom he delegated his problem.

'You've got three days!' he told them. 'In three days' time I want a firm recommendation.'

Bucholz and Schroeder warmed to their task and the unexpected excitement which the new campaign of terror promised them.

At the end of the allotted three days they reported to von Sahlenburg, Bucholz carrying a field map case on the talc overlay of which a red circle had been boldly drawn.

Von Sahlenburg looked up from his desk as they saluted, smiling at his visitors because he knew why they had come and, also, because he invariably felt warmly towards his new and rather special aides.

'All right! So you've decided on a location. Let me see where and why.'

Bucholz placed the open map case in front of the general. There was only one word within the red circle. That was St-Honor-sur-Clair.

That meeting didn't last long. Bucholz was quick to state the many and varied advantages of selecting an isolated target area such as this holiday village; all of which conformed to von Sahlenburg's original brief.

When he had finished the general leaned back in his chair and his smile widened.

'Good! Good!' he said with enthusiasm. 'Couldn't be better

if we plan to make our mark for once and for all.' He switched his eyes from one to the other. 'So how soon can you be ready?'

Schroeder answered, 'Almost immediately, sir! We've already worked out the details. We reckon that the entire operation should be over within a few hours.'

'Then, tomorrow?'

'Certainly, if that is what you wish, though we would prefer an afternoon start which would leave the following morning to clear up in daylight rather than have to work through the night.'

'Good thinking! No German casualties, eh? Fine! Then tomorrow afternoon it shall be. I'll inform the generalfeldmarschall, just for the record, though I suppose he's got enough on his mind right now.'

Shroeder took a step back, preparing to salute and leave, but Bucholz put in, 'Would I be right in thinking, sir, that on this occasion, too, you'd like an officer of field-rank to be present at St-Honor? Just as an observer, of course?'

Von Sahlenburg agreed at once.

'Please yourself, Kurt,' he replied easily. 'If you'd like a day out and you hate these bloody French peasants as much as I do, then go ahead! I'm sure Jurgen will be glad of your company.'

The only disappointed officer in Number 2 Panzergrenadier Company was Untersturmfuhrer Werner Odermatt who had anticipated he would be retained as company commander. He recalled his vow in the Fôret d'Ivres of a personal vendetta against French civilians and hoped that reverting to platoon commander wouldn't restrict his intent.

The Abbé Eugene Fournier pedalled happily along the narrow, winding lane which led from the neighbouring village of Aumont to St-Honor, a distance of eight kilometres. This was a journey which, since his ministry had been extended four years earlier, he had had to make every morning to say Mass.

But he didn't mind the trip at all. Not even in winter! It broadened his horizons – at least as far as Aumont, he often joked. The exercise did his liver good and he'd also found himself a lot of new friends in 'the little village down the road'.

Abbé Fournier was a great big, huggy-bear of a man with a grey-streaked beard as heavy as a thatch, sparkling blue eyes and a smile which lit up his entire face whenever he came upon a member of his flock. He also pedalled his ramshackle bicycle with the aggression and power of a rugger forward, so that the near-bald tyres kicked up continuous spurts of dust as he sped along.

But, today, he was loitering, revelling in the freshness of the morning. The sun had just broken through and the steady drizzle which had hampered the outward journey had given way to intermittent sunshine and the promise of a bright afternoon.

He glanced heavenwards at the rapidly expanding patch of blue. So it was going to be a fine day, after all. Thank you, Lord! Of course, he'd known all along that *le bon Dieu* wouldn't let the village down on a day such as this!

And why?

Because today was Wednesday and, more importantly, this was to be the children's sports day at St-Honor. The Champ de Foire had already been decorated with flags and a tent had been erected where the prizes were to be displayed. The athletics tracks, the long jumps, the high jumps had been marked out in whitewash on the freshly mown grass and, perhaps even at this moment, Louise Boisard from the *patisserie* and Marc Gauvrit from the Hotel de la Poste would be setting up tables of sweets, cakes and fruity drinks to help give the kiddies a day to remember.

It was good! Everything was good!

The abbé leaned over his handlebars to put more pressure on the pedals as the gradient steepened above the Clair Valley. Here, the puddles in the road were drying and the birds in the hedgerows were bursting into song at the sight of the sun.

But then a sudden frown crossed the abbés forehead and he ceased pedalling, head turning, listening. His frown deepened.

From back down the lane in the direction of Aumont he had caught the surge of automobile engines. Heavy engines, it seemed. Trucks? He pulled on the brake lever and squealed to a halt, concentrating. Military trucks? Possibly troop transporters!

Germans?

He felt his jaw tightening and a raw dryness came to his mouth. Why should German troops be heading towards St-Honor? St-Honor of all places! There hadn't been more than a score of Germans in the village during the whole war and they'd been officers who'd called to sample the Hotel de la Poste's gourmet menu. Then why Germans now? And why so many as to warrant infantry transporters?

Yet the trucks appeared to be moving slowly. Could be they were part of a convoy heading north for the Normandy battle zones. There'd been a lot of talk in the village about German troop movements through the Unoccupied Zone, but there'd been no official confirmation. Could be though. The Allies were reported to be pushing south from the Baie de la Seine and most people seemed to think that the days of the Wehrmacht were already numbered.

Even so, this was no time to take chances and he pushed his bicycle through a gap in the hedge and found himself a hiding place behind a couple of bushes where he could watch the trucks go by.

Two minutes later, they came into view. There was a small armoured scout car some hundred and fifty metres ahead of the first truck. Its commander was sitting easily on top of the small turret lip with earphones clamped over a service cap, the long radio antenna waving behind his head. It was travelling at not more than forty kilometres an hour. Behind the third truck was a staff car obviously carrying officers and, behind that, seven more trucks spaced at intervals of about fifty metres and with a second scout car at the tail. The trucks were uncovered and each carried its complement of armed soldiers sitting on bench seats, wearing steel helmets and camouflage suits. They looked alert and very operational.

The Abbé Fournier crouched deeper into the bushes, watching the scout car puff black exhaust smoke as the driver dropped a gear for the gradient. He turned his attention to the leading trucks in which the soldiers appeared to be impatient, several of them craning their necks to peer ahead as though anticipating their destination.

It was then that the abbé recognised the insignia on the side of their helmets.

Waffen SS!

In St-Honor? But, why, dear Lord?

His eyes lifted to the sky.

A holiday atmosphere was already animating the villagers of St-Honor-sur-Clair. At the boys' school the headmaster, Max Durr, had given up all hopes of quelling the excitement of his seventy-four pupils and had told his staff to devote the rest of the morning to discussions on major international sporting events in which France had excelled during the pre-war years.

Similarly, at the girls' school across the other side of the Champ de Foire, young Mademoiselle Danielle Poitier had promoted a discussion on women in sport amongst her senior classes. Only the infants seemed to be following a normal curriculum, and most of them were dreaming of all the good things they were to have to eat at the afternoon's party.

There were also many visitors in the village. The Hotel de la Poste and the Hotel des Charmettes, which faced each other across the green expanse of the Champ de Foire, were full to capacity, totalling forty-three guests in all. Most of the people were assembling in the bars for pre-lunch aperitifs, some congregating at the wrought-iron tables beneath the blue and white striped awning of the Hotel de la Poste; others relaxing in comfortable cane chairs in the lounge of the Hotel Charmettes which was reputed to cater for the more mature citizens.

This was a scene far removed from the horrors and inconveniences of war and the reason why most of these pople had come to St-Honor.

There were twenty-odd people from Paris who, scared that the capital would, in the event of a German withdrawal, become a spite target for the Luftwaffe had sought the tranquillity of this part of rural France. Amongst them was old Christiane Reynaud who, up to a week earlier, had lived in a luxury flat along the Champs Elysées. She was eighty-nine and her spinster daughter who accompanied her was sixty-six; both determined to live out their lives without suffering the threat of German bombs dropped to kill and to maim in defeat and disillusionment.

There were six members of an angling club from Sézanne who had planned this trip as far back as 1938. Monsieur François Leblanc, also a Parisien, had brought his two sons aged five and seven and his daughter aged nine to spend the rest of the war with a cousin in St-Honor, only to return to Paris when the Germans had been driven as far east as the Rhine.

At the Hotel des Charmettes sat Roual Hines and three senior scouts from a troop in Lyon, prizewinners in departmental fieldcraft exercises, come for three days to enjoy and prepare a paper on the flora and fauna of St-Honor. There was Louise Dubois, aged seventy-two from Angoulême who had a
104

fixation that the Americans would break from the Baie de la Seine and strike due south for the Côte d'Azur, laying waste to Angoulême en route. There were Doctor Emil Boeáux and his wife, also a doctor and both retired, who were seeking a new home somewhere along the Clair river.

There were also many other visitors about the village. At the presbytery, Odile, Abbé Fournier's young sister, who had taken a week from her secretarial job in Moulins to spend a short holiday with her brother. Elisabeth Landais' two grown-up sons had come north from Marseilles where they worked in the shipyards under the German *Rélève* plan. There were also groups of refugees from Alsace-Lorraine in temporary accommodation, mostly in outlying farms and hamlets.

School ended promptly at noon and the children dashed to their homes, ready to come racing back to the Champ de Foire in under half an hour, having eaten and changed into Sunday suits and summer dresses. They crowded at the clean white tapes which marked out the sports arena, eyes pivoting expectantly to a small stage which had been built beneath the trees on the southern side overlooking the river. During the afternoon a brass band would be arriving from Aumont. Later, in the evening, there would be dancing and the coloured fairy lights strung across the lower branches of the trees would be switched on. For the adults there would be wine, beef bread rolls and a special tobacco ration. For the children there would be sweets, cakes and more fruit drinks.

This was an increasingly happy crowd for, along with the children, there had also arrived in the village young farm workers of both sexes, taking a few hours off-duty until the evening milking.

It was the Abbé Eugene Fournier who sounded the alarm concerning the approach of the German column.

He telephoned the mayor, Victor Baraffe, at the *mairie* from Hugo Jacques' farm. The stunned Baraffe had found difficulty in assimilating what the abbé was telling him, seriously considering whether the priest had suddenly gone out of his mind. Eventually, convinced, he sank into a chair face bloodless, clutching his chest as sudden vicious pains struck him. Baraffe was not a young man and his heart had never been strong. He supposed he should be taking some action. But what? Dash out into the Champ de Foire yelling that the SS were just round the corner? Risk a panic?

He recalled a middle-aged woman named Nicole Grondin arriving in the village only three days ago. She'd come from a place called Talmont-les-deux-Ponts and had been quick to tell what horrors the SS were alleged to have committed there. Some of the people of St-Honor had believed her, but others had not, thinking she was exaggerating merely to enhance her ego. Whey would the Germans want to ravage a peaceful place such as she described? they asked each other. Maybe they'd had a little Maquis trouble there. Could be! But there'd been nothing about it in the newspapers, nor on the German-controlled radio!

Mayor Victor Baraffe's memory got a second jolt as he then recalled that there were two men staying at the Hotel de la Poste who, in line with custom, had reported an association with the Franc Tireurs et Partisans! Dazed, he went out into the street. These were tight-lipped, humourless men, he remembered, who'd refused point-blank to give him more than their aliases; Yves Durrain and Pierre Tessier. Baraffe had no alternative other than to let it go at that. Whilst there had never been any guerilla activity either in St-Honor or any of the neighbouring hamlets, he had been aware that, from time to time, the Maquis had made some use of its isolated position to plan anti-Wehrmacht operations and reform their units. No one had ever objected to that because these men had always given aliases and had seldom stayed in the village for more than forty-eight hours at a time.

Baraffe was halfway to the Hotel de la Poste when the distant rumble of heavy vehicles reached his ears. His heart began to pound again and pains seared across his chest with an unbearable intensity until his consciousness slipped away and he collapsed, face-down, on the pavement and still a hundred metres from the Champ de Foire.

In the Hotel de la Poste restaurant, Armand Guerineau and Marius Combin were also quick to hear the trucks. They looked across the table at each other with troubled eyes. Boches! These could only be Boches and that didn't make any sense at all.

Not in St-Honor-sur-Clair!

The SS arrived a little after one-thirty. Half the column roared straight through the village to the western perimeter, where they swung about and headed back into the centre, whilst the

106

rest of them closed off the main street and the bridge over the Clair river.

The panzergrenadiers sprang to the ground as soon as the transporters drew to a halt. These were young men, fit and healthy looking, wearing camouflage combat uniforms and armed with machine guns, machine pistols and self-loading rifles. Then, spurred by the raucous commands of their NCOs, they speedily surrounded the village and sealed all tracks and exits.

Initially, the population of St-Honor watched these operation with a cool interest rather than alarm. Could it be that the Boches were at last pulling out of this part of France? From Lyon? From St Etienne? From Vichy? Had the Allies broken out from their beachheads in Normandy and caused these bastards to go chasing back to defend their precious Fatherland?

Taking no chances, Guerineau and Combin unhurriedly refolded their napkins, eased back their chairs and quietly left the restaurant. Even though the villagers seemed to be taking the event calmly, they'd be fools to stick their necks out. Too late had the same meaning as death — when there were rampaging SS on the loose! Their own presence in St-Honor was a coincidence not to be ignored.

Their intention had simply been to meet other *réseau* leaders to discuss future plans and strategy, but now they could forget all about that and make their way back home to Viverois as soon as they found a way to slide through the SS cordon.

A few minutes later they left the hotel through a rear door and hurried across a number of gardens but had to dash for cover to an outbuilding when they spotted a detachment of SS combing the woods some distance ahead. It was at that moment they were able to identify the grenadiers' epaulette and cuff insignia, to see that these were soldiers from the same panzergrenadier regiment which had pillaged Talmont-les-deux-Ponts a week earlier. This knowledge gave Guerineau and Combin a keen personal involvement, making their escape all the more urgent if they were to warn the Maquis what the SS had in mind for St-Honor.

On their way to the Champ de Foire, the soldiers picked up the swooning mayor and slapped him back into awareness, ordering him to summon the town crier. This he did and old Henri Lapointe came stumbling painfully on to the Champ de

Foire, where he was told by an SS officer to beat his drum and announce that the entire population and all visitors were to assemble immediately, bringing their identity papers with them.

As at Talmont, this announcement caused a temporary lift in morale. They forced themselves to believe that, despite their show of strength, the SS were going to conduct nothing more frightening than an identity check. But, very quickly, the SS began to get impatient. They bustled people out of their homes at bayonet point, urging them down the street with blows from rifle butts if they were too ill or too old to move quickly enough. Those who collapsed were left to lie where they had fallen, until a following section came along to kick them to their feet and get them moving again.

To the people of St-Honor this had suddenly become a terrifyingly new experience; but to Armand Guerineau and Marius Combin, still lying low in the outbuilding, it was a standard form of procedure they had witnessed a score of times. Neither were armed, for to be found in possession of a handgun by the SS was to volunteer for immediate execution. All they could do was watch the barbarism without raising a hand.

About three hundred people had been herded into the Champ de Foire when trucks began to arrive from outlying farms and cottages, bringing others whom Untersturm-fuhrer Werner Odermatt's Number 3 Platoon had been ordered to collect. These people had already been subjected to considerable pressure for most of the women were weeping whilst their menfolk stood silently beside them, pale-faced, confused and helpless. Odermatt had wasted no time in beginning his promised personal vendetta against French civilians. At the Buton farm he had shot and killed René Buton simply because the farmer had been unwilling to leave his cattle wandering loose about the farmyard.

'If it's only an identity check,' he had reasoned good-humouredly, 'then, surely, you've got time to let me leave things tidy.'

But Odermatt, suddenly and unaccountably tense and white-faced, had pulled out his Luger automatic and shot him through the heart. In the hysterical screaming from Buton's wife, Marie, and his two small daughters, Elaine and Monique, even Odermatt's platoon-sergeant, Unterscharfuhrer Jacob

Kuhn, had frowned apprehensively at this first cold-blooded killing at St-Honor. Odermatt noticed and had immediately become even more aggressive and sent the platoon bustling through the outbuildings where they unearthed two sixteen-year-old boys, whom they harried into the truck at bayonet-point.

At the Daleau farm which skirted the tiny Lac Savin they merely dropped old Mimi Daleau into the water, wheelchair and all. There was no point in attempting to lift that on to a truck, Odermatt said, and they drove off with bubbles still rising from the drowning old lady and the rest of the Daleau family stunned and sickened into silence.

At the Bodard house they found a birthday party in progress and the children playing their games on the freshly mown lawn. Amongst them were a number of Alsatian refugees who began crying and screaming the instant the SS drew up. One small boy with not-so-old memories triggering his panic, fled headlong down the garden path when one of the grenadiers lifted his rifle and took a potshot at him as though he were sniping game. The child catapulted into the air under the force of the heavy-calibre bullet which struck him low in the back. Then, when Madame Bodard rounded on the man, screaming and clawing, he killed her too. Odermatt nodded his silent approval at such speedy reaction and the grenadier grinned as he jerked another round into the breech, kicking the ejected cartridge case high into the air before it touched the ground, indicating to the officer the lightning speed of his reflexes.

The trucks trundled into the Champ de Foire, lifting the tapes which had been laid for the children's sports, dragging them into the centre of the square.

There, the SS dropped the tailgates and yelled for their prisoners to get down.

'*Schnell*! *Schnell*!' they shouted, bustling them forward to join those already assembled. Some were clutching identity papers, others crying and fearing reprisals because the SS hadn't given them time to collect theirs.

At that point, the Abbé Eugene Fournier rode into the centre on his ancient bicycle. During the rest of his journey back to the village his mind had been in turmoil. Whilst he'd managed to phone a warning to Victor Braffe, he'd immediately realised that there was insufficient time for the mayor to take any positive action. There'd been no chance at all of him marshalling the few village cars and trucks and driving the women and children out of St-Honor. Had he had even an hour, then perhaps something could have been done, But, as it was, there'd been no time at all!

Now he stared, disbelieving, at the scene in the Champ de Foire: tight little groups of near-hysterical women, distraught men and young SS panzergrenadiers running wild amongst them, shoving and clubbing them into lines, bawling obscenities. A number of young women with small children, some of them also cradling babies in their arms, were hurried to the perimeter to collect more children who had assembled there to watch the sports. These infants had cheered at the unexpected arrival of the German soldiers, thinking this to be an added surprise and a part of the afternoon's fun.

The abbé looked about him, worried, seeking an officer. But when, eventually, he approached Untersturmfuhrer Werner Odermatt, the officer despatched a couple of men from his Platoon HQ to escort him to the lines of men.

Sturmbannfuhrer Kurt Bucholz and Hauptsturmfuhrer Jurgen Schroeder watched developments from their Mercedes-Benz staff car with one of the two armoured scout cars drawn up either side. They sat comfortably in the rear seat, impressed at the smoothness with which the grenadiers worked; gratified to see the degree of panic already instilled into the villagers.

Schroeder had remarked, 'It would have done von Sahlenburg good to have watched this!' At which Bucholz had replied laconically, 'And old Walter Keitel, too, I'd say!'

The men were made to sit in three rows on the east side of the Champ de Foire facing a row of houses and the Hotel de la Poste. They were warned that if they turned their heads they'd be shot, after which a section of grenadiers fired bursts from their Schmeiser machine pistols to prove they weren't fooling.

Whilst these moves were taking place, the women and children were led away. There were no opportunities for last minute farewells, no hysterics. The women just moved on, carrying their babies, pushing prams and leading their older children by the hand towards the little church with its squat steeple at the western end of the village. Some wept silently into their handkerchieves whilst others, close to collapse, had to be half-carried by their friends, most of them accepting that they were unlikely ever to see their loved ones again.

Schroeder watched the procession disappear before he opened the car door and stepped out on to the tarmac. He wore no cap and the breeze which had stirred into life after the morning's rain tugged at his short-cropped hair. He scowled into the sun, beckoning to Odermatt who came running at the command.

'Form those men into something like order, Untersturm-fuhrer!' he said curtly. 'Three distinct lines. Then make a count!'

'Sir!'

Odermatt strode rapidly back into his platoon group telling himself angrily that if Schroeder was supposed to have taken over the command of Number 2 Company, then he should be organising things himself instead of playing the high ranking staff officer.

A few minutes later, Schroeder addressed the hostages in moderately good French. There was no hint of aggression in his tone, which indicated a sharp contrast with the conduct of the grenadiers. He might well have been addressing a ladies' luncheon meeting in his home town of Ulm/Donau.

'Now listen, you men! You all know as well as I do why this parade is necessary. We haven't come here this afternoon to waste either our time or yours. The fact is that information has been received from reliable sources that the Maquis have a secret store of arms, ammunition and explosives hidden some-where in this village. Probably dropped to them by the American Air Force. So! If you want to get this business over with as quickly as we do, then all you've got to do is come forward and tell us where it is. There will be no personal incriminations. The identity of men volunteering such informa-tion will be kept secret. All right?'

There Schroeder paused, smiling amiably along the three ranks, raising his eyebrows, expressing surprise that no one rushed forward with the information.

In the outbuilding, from which a good third of the Champ de Foire was visible, Armand Guerineau shook his head sadly at Marius Combin. These bastard SS officers knew for a fact there had been neither Maquis nor guerilla equipment parachuted within tens of kilometres of St-Honor. That was the very reason they'd picked this village! Because they'd known from the start that there'd be no chance of the Maquis springing a sudden attack on their grenadiers.

111

Schroeder went on, 'Of course, I can understand your reluctance to come forward with the rest of the village looking on. What I propose to do, therefore, is to split you up into a number of small groups and send you to different parts of the village which my officers have already selected. You will appreciate that unless you give us the information we want, then we must search every building before we leave St-Honor!'

He looked speculatively over the hostages before turning again to Odermatt who despatched his grenadiers amongst them, detailing them into five groups of roughly the same number.

The men shambled off between their SS guards with rising apprehension, knowing that each and every move which the SS made weakened their own position. For the first time there rose amongst them secret fears that they might be taken away and shot, but none dared voice that opinion. It was better that they should wait and see what developed, for there was nothing they could do right now under the SS guns.

Guerineau watched a party of about sixty men approach the outbuilding from the Champ de Foire. This batch was new to him. They must have been at the south side of the square and wide of the angle of his vision from the small window.

They appeared to be heading for a garage he had noticed fifty metres or so farther along the street. He beckoned to Combin who came to stand beside him, also watching the straggling column. Many of them were weeping, others walked with their heads turned in the direction of the church where they believed their women and children had been taken.

Guerineau and Combin were grim-faced. There was no doubt at all that this was to be an SS reprisal for the bombing in the Fôret d'Ivres and the murder of the two senior officers whom the Maquis had tortured to death. But this was just another phase in the Maquis' relentless fight with the Boches. There was nothing they could do about it now! The Maquis would still have to go on killing Germans. They still had to take what pressure they could off the Allied armies holding the Normandy beachheads. And that not only here in the Massif Centrale, but all over France, both Occupied and Unoccupied Zones. There were identical situations in Belgium, Holland, Luxemburg, Norway; everywhere where free men were continuing their fight with the Boches. It was sad that innocent civilians had to die, too. That was the bitter pill! But the only

112

real weapon the Germans had against Resistance fighters was reprisals and they'd use it to the end!

They were turning away from the window when the door suddenly crashed open and three SS grenadiers were standing holding MP-40 Schmeiser machine pistols. The man in the centre of the group guffawed, 'Christ! But look what we've found here!' But a sturmann came bustling up behind them, impatient and irritable.

'Who let these men through?' he demanded to know. Then, 'All right! So move 'em!'

He made a sweeping gesture with his hand, yelling at Guerineau and Combin to put their hands on top of their heads and to catch up with the column out there. '*Schnell*! *Schnell*!'

The three grenadiers wasted no time in reacting to their section leader's orders and struck the Frenchmen across the shoulders with their weapons, bundling them through the door and out into the street, hurrying them after the hostages who had passed seconds earlier.

By the time Guerineau and Combin reached the garage, the first arrivals were making space inside, trundling out a couple of old cars, some pieces of farm machinery and a flat-cart. These they left in the street as the SS continued to beat them, crowding them back into the building.

At this point about half the grenadiers were marched away, evidently to seek more escaped civilians, leaving only five of the section positioned across the workshop entrance, toying with their machine pistols.

The hostages were still eyeing them nervously but, now this mad chase along the street from the Champ de Foire was over, they believed that much of the heat had been taken from the incident. And, as a result, they began to feel easier. Nobody had believed a bloody word the SS hauptsturmfuhrer had said about village involvement with the Maquis. But, on the other hand, if the Boches had been given that kind of information, then they could be said to have a legitimate reason for a house-to-house search. When they'd done that and found nothing, then they'd probably accept that they'd been misinformed and clear off.

Probably with the exception of Guerineau and Combin, none expected to be shot. The younger men were more worried about possible deportation under the *Relêve* scheme than of anything else – apart from the constant nagging fear for the women and children of the village. But, they told themselves, they'd be safe so long as they were in the church. Pity, though, the abbé hadn't gone with them instead of insisting that he should remain with the men.

So those in the garage milled anxiously about the oil-stained, concrete floor, smiling wanly whenever they caught the eye of a close friend or neighbour, increasingly aware of the silence which had descended upon the village during the past few minutes Their alarm grew as they watched the grenadiers clip loaded magazines into their Schmeiser machine pistols, laughing and joking in a language they didn't understand.

A red flare suddenly soared into the sky, fired from the direction of the Champ de Foire. The guards braced themselves and spread out equidistantly across the entrance to the workshop.

The Frenchmen held their breaths, paling, but Guerineau and Combin threw themselves flat on the floor the instant they realised what was about to happen. From somewhere farther along the street there came a burst of machine gun fire and, with it, the five grenadiers opened up at point-blank range into the bodies of the men in the garage.

Guerineau sprawled with his arms about his head as though they might protect him from the hail of 9mm bullets which ricochetted on all sides from the walls and floor. The air became thick with fine dust as men began to fall around him. His first thoughts were for Marius Combin, but he didn't dare to lift his head. There arose a pandemonium of screaming amongst the coughing and more bodies fell on him.

Seconds later, the shooting ceased abruptly as though a command had been given. With it, much of the screaming also subsided, the men accepting death as their life-blood streamed from them; the anxieties of a few minutes earlier dissolving into nothing.

There followed a succession of single shots and he couldn't tell whether they were from pistols or machine guns; but it was clear that the grenadiers were moving amongst the bodies, killing off any which still moved or made a noise. Guerineau steeled himself as, through a fractionally open eye, he glimpsed jackboots kicking over bloodied faces, moving from one corpse to another.

Any second now!

He braced his muscles to take the thud of the bullet which he

114

knew must come and it was then that he found he could no longer move his left hand. He supposed the warmth suffusing his upper arm must be blood. Yet it didn't seem important. Unaccountably, the moaning around him had ceased and so had the shooting. So what happened now?

He lay still, anxious about Marius Combin whom he feared must have perished with the other sixty-odd men in that garage. At the clomp of more heavy boots, he again half-opened an eye. The SS-men were coming back in strength and dragging bedding and mattresses with them. Others carried bales of straw from the corn merchant next door, piles of newspapers taken from the houses. They brought in a child's wooden cot, a small chest of drawers, several kitchen chairs which they piled on top of the bodies.

From somewhere far off a radio began to screech out jazz, probably Guerineau thought, relayed through one of the truck or scout car systems. It was loud, coarse music, interspersed with occasional bursts of Schmeiser fire and the more distant cries of women.

It was as the grenadiers left that Guerineau found he was not the only survivor, for muffled cries began to rise from the pile of bodies. He half-turned his head. There was rich dark blood dripping from a shattered skull on to the concrete floor, centimetres from his face. Beyond he could see a man lying prone across the top of the pile, still breathing. He attempted to shift himself from under those sprawled over his limbs, pinning him to the floor, but he was hampered by his wounded left arm which had neither strength nor feeling. He had covered no more than a metre when the SS returned.

They produced matches and began setting alight the mattresses and straw which caught fire immediately, sending black smoke curling up to the rafters. The grenadiers were laughing and joking noisily amongst themselves as they moved about the garage with their fire-brands. When the flames began to lick about his face and the pain became unbearable, Guerineau kicked the bodies from him. He scrambled to his feet, expecting the fusillade which would send him reeling dead back into the heap of bodies. His hair was on fire and he beat at the flames frenziedly with his good hand, barely sensing the shrivelling of his fingernails.

When he realised that the grenadiers had left, he looked out into the street to see them moving into the direction of the

115

Champ de Foire — probably, he thought, to find a new place of execution for those who, so far, had been allowed to live.

As the flames, whipped by the breeze, spread up the side wall he went back into the workship seeking Combin. But there was no sign of him. He flung open the door at the back of the room on the chance of finding an escape route. There was a man already there. He was an old man, lying bleeding on the stone floor, who had given himself up to death and had sought only to escape the final agonies of being burned alive.

Guerineau breathed hard, carrying his wounded arm in his right hand, the first twinges of pain from the fire searing his face and head. He went back into the workshop where he began to move the bodies so that he could see their faces.

Eventually, he found Marius Combin, who appeared to have caught the full blast of a Schmeiser magazine. Several of his ribs had splattered through his shirt and his chest looked like one great swamp of blood and shredded flesh.

Guerineau sighed.

So that was that!

It was as sad as it was ironic that, after the countless risks which Combin had taken fighting with the Maquis, he should perish in such a haven as St-Honor. Ironic, too, that he should die without firing a shot in return! Shot like some stray dog without either dignity or identity.

Guerineau looked over the rest of the corpses and, momentarily a rising anger contorted his face and clouded his eyes, but he threw it from him, striding back into the small room behind the workship where he found that the old man had died.

He nudged open an opaque-glass window, not knowing what lay on the other side, then climbed on top of a wooden crate to peer through the slit he'd made. There was a long, narrow stretch of uncultivated land running parallel to the gardens behind the houses along that same street. He forced the window as wide as it would open and painfully eased himself through the gap, dropping head-first into clumps of nettles and dock on the outside. There he lay for several minutes breathing heavily, conscious of blood draining from his fingertips, sniffing his own flesh roasting.

He knew that he had to move and move quickly if he was to stand any chance at all of escaping from this village, but it was only when a pandemonium of screaming arose from the direction of the Champ de Foire that he levered himself to his knees and then to his feet.

As he moved alongside the hedge away from the garage the air became thick with the brittle crackle of burning timber and the din from the gramophone still churning out its amplified jazz. Columns of smoke also began to rise on all sides, which caused him some indecision as to which direction he should take.

At the far end of the garden he found a part of the fencing was down, obviously demolished by workers to provide them with a short-cut from the lane to the garage. Ahead was a spread of open grassland. He glanced quickly in both directions and then took a chance, sprinting to a belt of tall trees beyond. Again, he anticipated a burst of automatic fire, but none came and he sank into a dry ditch breathing harder but with no additional injuries.

Only then did he look over himself and find he was splattered from head to foot with blood – and only a little of his own. Most had drained from the bodies in the garage, and that could be an advantage if it ever became necessary to play dead again. Meanwhile, he'd try to orientate himself to discover his position in the village. Pity he hadn't visited St-Honor earlier, for there'd been no time since his arrival late the previous evening to take a look around.

He found a gap in a yew hedge across the lane and squeezed through it into a large meadow. He accepted there was little immediate chance of him getting out of the village for, by now, the SS would have sealed off all roads in line with their routine practice of complete isolation. Static detachments would be reinforced by mobile patrols using the infantry transporters. The most sensible thing he could do right now was to lie low and take no chances until nightfall, even though that wouldn't be easy . . . for the degree of bloodletting and brutality indulged in by the SS indicated a 'no-survivors' campaign.

He began to work his way back in the direction of the Champ de Foire, keeping close to the hedges. There were no Germans to be seen and it appeared that most of those around the pre-selected execution centres were still mopping up, for he heard the intermittent rattle of automatic fire whilst the screaming of the imprisoned women rarely faltered.

Some minutes later he came upon what he guessed to be a main road through the village, though he could recall no identifiable landmarks. But, some distance farther along, he spotted a small cottage at the end of a cul-de-sac. Strung across a patch of lawn behind the house was a line of freshly laundered clothing flapping in the breeze.

Guerineau breathed a sigh of relief as he edged his way up to the cottage, stooping low beneath the window, pausing there to listen. As he'd anticipated, the place was deserted and he went on into the garden and took a couple of white summer dresses and a man's shirt from the washing line. He would have liked to have gone inside and cleaned himself up, but he daren't risk the SS returning to set fire to the place. His appearance didn't matter a damn, but he needed to take a look at his wounded left arm. There was no movement either of the hand or the fingers which hung at the end of the shattered wrist bone like dead things. He was also sensing nausea which he put down to shock and loss of blood, but by Christ he daren't faint!

He found a bucket which he half-filled at a pump in the garden and then took it along with the clothes from the line down the yew hedge to a copse which was three-quarters the distance back to the garage. This, he guessed, was the wisest thing to do for he'd noticed a thickening column of smoke rising from the garage workshop and the breeze was bringing with it the stench of burning human bodies. It indicated that, by this time, the SS could have moved farther afield to wreak more carnage. If he was right, then it might also be better to seek some other escape route from St-Honor; maybe by way of the church. If the SS had locked the women inside the church as they had at Talmont, there was a possibility that that side of the village could be free of them.

In the copse he put down the bucket and began to strip of his shirt and jacket, both stiff with congealed blood, flaking and brown. On his left arm, the linen of the shirt was stuck fast around the edges of the wound though blood still welled from its dark, hollow centre. He scooped up water in a cupped right hand, gulping feverishly, throwing back his head to let it run cool down his chest, then splashing more over his head and shoulders. With that, some of the nausea began to ebb and though the pain from the wound intensified at the exertion, he felt more able to cope with it.

Gingerly, then, he began to ease the shirt sleeve clear of the wound, his face contorted in pain, eyes dulled and rolling and turned to the sky whilst he persisted at peeling off the linen.

118

Centimetre by centimetre it came away until, with one quick snatch, it came free – whereupon he threw himself face-down in the grass, moaning and clawing at the ground in his agony.

Much more blood spurted from the wound without the coagulation and he sensed it running freely down his forearm again to drip off his finger ends. Yet he didn't move, scared of seeing the extent of his injury. He knew as well as the SS what kind of damage a 9mm bullet could do to human flesh and bone when fired at close range: a neat little hole where it had entered the body and a yawning, bloody gap at the other side where it had come out. That was about the best he could hope for – though God knew what he'd find!

It was another prolonged burst of machine gun fire from close at hand, followed by a crescendo of frantic screaming, that eventually caused him to move himself. Then he turned, looking down at his wound, and the fresh waves of nausea which immediately seized him had him toppling against the bushes. Jesus! He'd been prepared for the sight of raw flesh and even naked bone but, dear God, nothing so terrible as this!

At a first glance it appeared that he'd been hit by two or three bullets at the same time, close together in a tight cone of fire. The elbow had been shattered and all that remained holding the forearm on to the upper arm seemed to be white strings of arteries, guiders and sinew.

He shook his head in an attempt to clear the nausea then, on reflex, again dipped into the pail of water. He moved into a sitting position, staring not at the wound, but sightlessly at the ground in front of him, for the first time realising the hopelessness of his predicament. It had suddenly become clear to him that there wasn't a chance in hell of making it out of this village in one piece. With this kind of an injury he'd flake out before he'd covered a single kilometre – and that without him having to make a cross-country detour to dodge the SS!

His mind wandered hazily to the dead Marius Combin and he began to wonder who was the better off. If the SS found him now, they wouldn't give him much of an opportunity to die a dignified death, either! They'd probably have him stumbling round the Champ de Foire whilst they took potshots at him with their self-loading rifles; or they'd torture him into committing revolting obscenities against the women. That was the kind of reaction he could expect from such bastards – they wouldn't acknowledge a single failure without making the man responsible jump for it and, so far as he was concerned, without even suspecting his true identity!

The problem was that events had moved far too quickly since the sweeping victory of the Franc Tireurs et Partisans over the German 603rd Infantry Battalion at Talmont-les-deux-Ponts.

Since then a lot of people had died on both sides, and most of them SS, which had directly resulted in some pressure being taken off the Allied armies in Normandy. Even more than that: there were rumours that General George Patton's United States 3rd Army had the 2nd Free French Armoured Division spearheading their south-bound break through. With a little luck, the 32nd Panzer Division Waffen SS Uber Alles might bump headlong into the formation they needed to avoid at all costs for, undoubtedly, the Free French would by that time have been briefed by the Franc Tireurs et Partisans on the murders and wanton devastation here at St-Honor.

Guerineau took a deep breath and squared his shoulders. After all he'd been through he couldn't just give up and sit around waiting for death in this copse, could he? That would mean that Marius had died for nothing! He had to make his friend's sacrifice worthwhile if he couldn't do as much for his own! Then, perhaps some day, he'd have the courage to face Combin's wife, Louise, who'd loved her man to distraction.

A little stronger now he looked again at his wound, half-closing his eyes as a reflex defence against its severity. It wasn't even the kind of wound to which he could apply a tourniquet. If he tried, then there was a positive danger that the whole forearm might come away or, and just as bad, become gangrenous.

Using his teeth and his good hand he ripped one of the dresses into strips, making a huge swab which he placed inside the wound rather than on top. This he bound in tightly as close to a tourniquet as he dared, pinning it with a piece of twig which he'd filed to a point against a stone. He tore more strips, knotting them together into a single length. This he wound about his body, lashing the left forearm across his stomach, leaving much of the shattered elbow open to the air, hoping that the blood would be quick to coagulate as it had before. Then he bathed his upper body in what remained of the water, finally struggling into the shirt with its empty sleeve waving to and fro whenever he moved.

He began to feel fitter but, all the same, he sank back against a tree trunk, realising that with the passing of the nausea some of the urgency had also gone. There was no longer any need to attempt a quick escape. The SS would leave in their own good time and, eventually, there would be French people arriving who'd stumble upon the scene of the massacre and, in their horror, be quick to summon help. If need be he could wait till that happened.

He glanced at his watch.

Four-twenty.

In five hours or so it would be dark. He would think again, then. He found his eyelids drooping in a new weariness which was beginning to engulf his whole body which he didn't have either the strength or the will to resist.

Sturmbannfuhrer Kurt Bucholz and Hauptsturmfuhrer Jurgen Schroeder, unlike their predecessors Haller and Kaser, were not content to sit beneath the awning of a café-bar sipping pastis whilst their junior officers had all the fun. In contrast, they moved freely about the village, watching the SS act against the population. They strolled - unhurriedly, fully relaxed, in the middle of an escort of six riflemen, three carrying MP-40 Schmeiser machine pistols, three with MG-42 machine guns slung from their necks on webbing straps with shortened ammunition belts clipped into the breeches. The officers were, themselves, unarmed. Neither did they wear battle equipment as they wandered through the burning streets with the cries of the dying and wounded ringing in their ears.

This was a gesture which the other ranks appreciated. It helped provide authenticity and reality to the orders they were carrying out — certifying their action against the French civilians as justifiable and necessary. The junior officers appreciated this senior involvement, too. It gave their own prestige a boost within their commands, forging a platoon into a dedicated and single-minded team.

In addition to the garage where Guerineau and Combin had been taken, four other execution centres had also been established: a barn, a smithy, a bakery, and a small abattoir. The latter proved to be the most suitable for, there, the SS had slashed up the corpses with the butchering equipment they found lying about the place and sluiced the blood away along concrete channels provided for that purpose. Consequently, no effort had been made here to cremate the bodies. Instead, they had stacked them three and four deep alongside the freezer, as though somebody might need them again at some time or other.

Bucholz and Schroeder visited each execution site in turn. All five were still and silent, for the last to die had already passed on, or had been finished off with a shot from a Luger automatic. Only the bloodstained, bullet-scarred walls and the untidy piles of corpses burned beyond recognition, remained. These the officers inspected nonchalantly, ignoring the stench, nodding their approval to the NCOs and then leaving abruptly for them to get on with whatever they were doing.

On their way back to the Champ de Foire, Bucholz and Schroeder came across Untersturmfuhrers Wolfgang Sieloff and Werner Odermatt, standing together at the junction with the lane which led down to the Clair river. They sprang to attention and saluted the instant the senior officers came into view.

Schroeder greeted them with his usual bland good humour.

'Sieloff? Odermatt? I see you've had yourselves a busy day, huh?'

'Sir!'

They acknowledged together, in accord; but, only minutes previously, there had been a short fuse burning between them. Sieloff, who three days earlier had been shocked by what he had witnessed at Talmont-les-deux-Ponts, was both angry and outraged at the unrestrained killing and brutality perpetrated by the grenadiers here in St-Honor. He had said as much to Odermatt who, already despising Sieloff as a weak and ineffective officer, had curled his lip and claimed in so many words that he had personally killed twenty-three French civilians that very afternoon.

Sieloff had stared at him, disbelieving.

'You? Twenty-three? Surely not!'

Odermatt had come back at him, angry and disturbed that a brother SS officer should not look upon the day's brief in the same light as himself.

'Why not?' he demanded heatedly. 'Why not, for Christ's sake? Didn't you see our men die in those bloody woods at Vichy? Well? Didn't you? How do you expect the SS to react? To track down the Yank aircrews? Or the Maquis who tortured the location out of Haller? We don't have that amount of time, Sieloff! We've got to hit where we can and where it hurts most! Unsuspecting communities such as this will make the Maquis both think and remember. That should make sense to every officer and every grenadier in Number 2 Company!'

Sieloff had shaken his head sadly, but made no reply. What was the point of telling an out-and-out Nazi like Odermatt that these were innocent people who'd sought nothing in life other than to live a quiet existence in this placid valley in the sun? That sometimes the SS got themselves all screwed up. They'd got diseased inside and the doctrine they preached was often as warped as the mentality of their leaders.

Had Odermatt guessed that such was his opinion he'd probably have shot him there and then and brought his count of murders for the day up to twenty-four. There was something unnatural about the harsh set of Odermatt's jaw, the tightness of the skin over his cheekbones and the wild luminosity about his eyes. He'd probably enjoyed himself killing so many unarmed, innocent French people who had never knowingly set eyes on a member of the Maquis.

'There still seems to be a lot of noise coming from the church, Odermatt,' Schroeder observed in his quiet tone. 'Have you any idea what's going on down there?'

Odermatt shook his head.

'Can't say, sir! I've just come from the smithy up the road. Before that I was at the bakery.'

Schroeder nodded.

'Yes! Yes! Very commendable, Odermatt. But now go and have a look at the church, will you? We can't have such a noise going on all day, you know!'

'Sir!'

The women and children of St-Honor had been locked in the church from the time they had been separated from their menfolk. It was there they had heard the machine pistols of the execution squads. And there where, despite their hysterics and their screaming, they had somehow accepted the awful truth that their loved ones were dead and, in all probability, they'd never see even their bodies again.

Together with the children there was a total of over three hundred crowded into a tiny church built to take a congregation of less than two-hundred-and-fifty. Many of the children, who had come into the village from outlying farms and hamlets to take part in the afternoon's games, were without their

123

parents – who knew nothing of the massacre or even of the arrival of the SS. These were clustered, white-faced and fretful, around their teachers, the despair and distress of the women beyond their comprehension.

It was a little after 4 pm when Untersturmfuhrer Werner Odermatt and two rifle sections of his Number 3 Platoon approached the church. A section leader unlocked a small side door, two of his men carrying between them a crate of glass smoke grenades to which short-duration fuses had been attached and which trailed some metres from the crate. They pushed their way through the congestion of weeping women, the rottenfuhrer bludgeoning them aside with the butt of his machine pistol, whilst the grenadiers behind him hauled the crate into the middle of the nave. Then, unhurriedly, they applied matches to the fuses, waiting until they had burned to within a few centimetres of the grenades before running out of the building and locking the door again behind them.

Meanwhile, the rest of Odermatt's detachment had lined the western end of the church and, as the smoke grenades exploded, so they flung open the doors and emptied the magazines of their machine pistols into the screaming, hysterical, writhing mass of women and children. Then, as the shooting died to a ragged splatter of single shots they slammed shut the doors again, standing around in noisy groups waiting for the coughing and choking to indicate that their victims had died either from bullet wounds or from asphyxia from the grenades.

A quarter of an hour later they re-opened the main doors, letting out most of the smoke before moving inside, this time with Odermatt at their head. He ordered them to pile chairs, lengths of carpet and anything else combustible they could find on top of the heap of bleeding bodies. Then he called in a grenadier with a flame-throwing gun who squirted napalm on top of them. As it erupted in one single, deafening blast, so the grenadiers doubled back into the street, pausing only to lock the doors behind them.

Immediately there a rose a new and concerted pandemonium of screaming from both women and children. It was apparent that many had been feigning death when the grenadiers had fired their machine pistols into the crowd and that these were now being burned alive. Odermatt at once detailed his grenadiers to take up positions around the perimeter wall and train their weapons on the windows. Thus, whenever a demented, tortured woman's face appeared, it was instantly fired upon until it dropped, torn and bloodied, back inside.

It took half an hour for the three hundred women and children to die. Now the only sound from the church was the crackle of burning timber and the roar of flames about the rafters. Odermatt sent one of his rifle sections to make a final sweep of that part of the village adjacent to the church, checking on the houses which, so far, had escaped the conflagration. In their search they came upon a number of bedridden invalids whom they shot in their beds, and then set the mattresses on fire on the chance that the whole house might catch alight. Here and there a few people who, somehow, had managed to dodge the SS until this late hour were winkled out of roadside ditches, cellars and even sewer drains. They, too, were immediately shot and their bodies heaved into the nearest building which was then also burned.

By about 6 pm the fire was at its height with three-quarters of the buildings blazing, including the church and the two hotels in the Champ de Foire.

It was about this time, too, that Armand Guerineau awoke from his sleep of exhaustion.

Armand Guerineau lay back in the long grass and stared up at the sky through a moving canopy of leaves. He noticed that the sun had shifted a good way towards the west, which indicated that he must have slept for several hours. He was also listening to his blood pumping and thumping through his wound, causing him to reach over with his right hand to feel the condition of the bandage. There was a hard crust of dried blood which extended over the front of his shirt, but nothing seemed to be running wet. He breathed a sigh of relief. Miraculously the arteries were holding out. Had they not then, sooner or later, his body would have been taken from this copse and stacked with those of the other murdered Frenchmen. He levered himself up on his good elbow, testing his strength, but at once his vision swam and, carefully, he lowered himself back to the ground. It appeared that the sleep had done him little good. The wound had stiffened the entire left side of his body and sharp stabs of pain were beginning to shoot through his elbow with increasing regularity.

He glanced at his watch.

Six-fifteen!

So he'd slept for the best part of three hours and during the whole of that time the SS hadn't been near this copse; or, if they had, then they'd left him for dead. Anyway, from the amount of smoke weaving all around him it looked as though they intended to spend the night in the village. They still had that damned jazz music blaring out through amplifiers as loud as ever and, now and then, he could catch snatches of German voices, laughter and even singing. Evidently, the SS had been following their usual practice of looting the cognac. Under the circumstances, probably the best thing to do was lie low where he was until they decided to pull out. He'd have a better chance of staying alive here in this copse than he would roaming the streets seeking to escape.

So he lay back with his face again turned up towards the treetops, his mind refocusing on the killing of Marius Combin in the garage not a couple of hundred metres from this spot. He could have wept for Marius. Murder by young SS thugs was no death for a man of Combin's calibre. Combin who'd fought at his side with the Franc Tireurs et Partisans way back in the dark, desperate days of 1940. Combin, who'd been one of the few Maquis fighters to have escaped from the Dachau death camp. Combin, who'd had personal experience of an SS Konzentrationslager and had used that experience to inspire all new recruits to the *réseau*.

'Do you have a glimmer of an idea of the kind of tortures and humiliations your countrymen are suffering as you sit around here?' he often demanded, his voice rising in the tension which his mental images immediately produced. 'And do you know what's waiting for those poor devils? Waiting for them after they've been reduced to walking skeletons, whipped, beaten and desperately ill? After they've lived on pig swill for months? Suffered scabies, blood-poisoning, dysentry, typhoid and God knows what other diseases and with no drugs, no medical attention, not even rest! Can you guess what the SS has waiting for them? Of course you can! Death! Death! Death! The SS already have death laid on because for them it can't come too quickly. They want to make room for fitter people fresh from occupied villages such as yours. And what kind of deaths? I'll tell you because I've seen it all for myself. First hand! Death by slow asphyxiation from diesel

126

truck exhausts extended through holes in the sides of wooden huts. That kind of death! Then cremation in great ovens with bodies piled seven or eight deep. Yes! Boys like yourselves from good homes have to die like vermin because the SS master-race wants it that way! Yes! And that's why this *réseau* always has the bastards in its sights! Always! The Maquis can never tire! Kill-a-Boche-a-Day...!'

Combin would then go on to describe his own experience at the Konzentrationslager. How the train pulled into the vast reception area of Dachau. A long train of up to fifty cattle trucks into which over 6,000 men, women and children had been herded and of whom a thousand were found to be dead when the doors of the trucks were eventually unlocked.

He described how, behind small windows criss-crossed with thick barbed wire, the faces of young children could be seen, eyes wide in stark terror, their pale, thin faces begrimed and streaming tears. Then, as the doors were flung open, SS guards ran amongst their prisoners herding them into line with leather whips.

They were ordered to remove all clothing, including artificial limbs, dentures and spectacles, and were handed pieces of string with which to tie their boots together. Money, valuables, rings, watches were confiscated by the SS guards who stuffed them into canvas holdalls. They gave no receipts, moving quickly down the lines and whipping any person who had the courage to protest.

Shortly afterwards they were led to a long, low wooden building marked with a sign: 'Baths and Disinfestation', in front of which women and girls were halted to have their hair clipped down to a stubble before being hurried on to join the rest of the column.

At that stage, an SS officer had addressed them, informing them that the men were to be detailed to build houses, roads and do general pioneering work about the camp whilst the women would be employed on housework in the staff quarters, sewing, making repairs to uniforms, or working in the kitchens. Right now they were to get themselves cleaned up! There would also be infection-destroying treatment and they were advised to breathe deeply into the sprays, for sound inhaling was the best way to prevent contagious diseases.

So the column was led up the steps into the death chambers, most of the people believing what the SS officer had told them and going willingly with neither question nor complaint. But, inside, they found more SS guards with whips who crowded them together until the building was crammed solid with people. Then the doors were closed, leaving the other prisoners standing naked outside, patiently waiting.

At the rear of the building a diesel truck, from which the exhaust had been connected to a hose leading to holes in the floor, was started. The engine turned at medium revs for over half an hour, at the end of which all the people inside were dead. Then Jewish workers opened doors at the other side of the building and went inside, where bodies were still standing erect in death for there had been insufficient room for them to fall or even to lean.

These workers, long experienced in their tasks, tossed out the bodies wet with sweat and urine, the legs soiled with faeces and menstrual blood. More workers appeared to check the mouths of the dead which they prised open with metal hooks. Others inspected the anus and genital organs seeking money, diamonds and gold. Then, finally, before the mass cremation, dentists hammered out gold teeth, bridges and crowns . . .

Marius Combin had witnessed such inhumanity and yet he had escaped, eventually to make his way home to Paris where he had reported to the Franc Tireurs et Partisans *réseau* and immediately volunteered for guerilla service.

It had been three months later that Armand Guerineau and he had met, when Combin's hate had still been running high and when there were fears amongst his compatriots that his wild lust for killing German soldiers could put their own security at risk. Guerineau had helped ease some of the man's sudden and almost maniacal tensions, but months had passed before Combin had been allowed to carry a gun. Even then, there had been occasions when Guerineau had held on to the bullets until seconds before his commitment!

It had been in January of this year that Marius Combin had finally been given a command of his own. It was ironic that their first full-scale action action together should have been the incident at Talmont-les-deux-Ponts which, ultimately was to result in the rape of St-Honor and Combin's death. Guerineau shook his head sadly. Combin had always insisted that one day he'd die in front of a German firing squad. Perhaps he had. But he hadn't meant along with some seventy-odd innocent Frenchmen whose only crime had been to live in the same village.

As more time passed, Guerineau began to get restless, spurred on by a burning thirst. Maybe he could stick it out here in the copse for another few hours, he told himself, but there was little chance of him staying until tomorrow morning. By that time his thirst would have become unbearable and, besides, his wound needed changing unless he was prepared to risk gangrene. He decided he should move now — whilst the SS were celebrating and clapping each other on the back for the bravery they'd demonstrated to the people of St-Honor that afternoon. From the amount of noise coming from the Champ de Foire it was apparent that many were already drunk and unlikely to react to distant footsteps, even if they heard them. Anyway, there were animals roaming freely about the village; dogs cowering and frightened, whimpering for their dead masters; cats and poultry seeking food.

He slowly got to his knees, gulping air as more nausea seized him, dragging himself to his feet with the branch of a tree and moving gingerly across the narrow width of the copse, testing his balance and the strength of his limbs. Five minutes later, he was standing amongst the perimeter bushes, looking out over his immediate surroundings.

Directly ahead, at the end of a stretch of garden, stood a fairly large house, more affluent-looking than its neighbours. If there had been random looting here, then surely the SS would have ransacked the biggest houses as a priority, since they'd consider the plunder to be worthwhile. But it was also likely they'd be coming back later to give it a second going over. He pondered on that logic and the set off boldly down the garden.

Nothing happened. Not even a shout — but all the same he found himself hunching his shoulders as he closed the distance in case a sudden burst of small-arms fire came his way. As he reached the back entrance to the house, his morale lifted. Not only had he made his first bound undetected, but he was also beginning to feel stronger. His wound still hurt like hell . . . but . . . the caricature of a smile touched his lips as he read the nameplate on the door.

So this wasn't the back door to the house as he'd imagined! It was the door of a doctor's surgery! The nameplate read: Dr François de Larocque — a name he knew to be commonplace in St-Honor. What luck!

He pushed through a small waiting room into the surgery

beyond and there he paused, staring at a photograph in an oak frame on top of a secretaire. He frowned as he puzzled. He'd seen that face somewhere before! Somewhere! And then he recalled the old man who had crawled into the small room behind the garage workshop to die that morning. That man had been Dr François de Larocque!

There was water, antiseptic and bandages, if not drugs, and he took his time stripping off his makeshift dressing and then bathing the wound. It still looked frightening, but not as vicious as it had earlier in the day. It was no longer pouring blood and with most of the congealed blood washed from around the wound, the pain appeared to be bearable. Carefully, he re-strapped his left arm across his stomach and went upstairs, where he found himself a clean shirt. There he also washed his face and combed his hair, before going down again to the kitchen where he drank freely from a pitcher of water cooling on a stone slab. He found some bread, cheese and a flagon of wine which he took into the parlour at the front of the house where he sat at the window, gazing out pensively on to the deserted road with not an SS grenadier in sight. Yet the SS had been here. There was no doubt about that. Most of the drawers had been dragged from the furniture and their contents strewn across the floors of the rooms he'd seen. He wondered what they'd found to send home to their doting parents – these brave sons of the Third Reich? A few much-loved souvenirs, cherished from those long-gone days when the family had enjoyed their freedom. Bastards! No punishment could be too cruel for the Waffen SS! Please God he'd live to see the time they paid for today's work!

He settled back in an easy chair, realising for the first time that this was the view which Dr de Larocque must have looked upon for the past four or five decades. It was fitting, therefore, that from this window there were no signs of the SS devastation. The narrow ribbon of road, with its tarmac bubbled and pitted along its edges and the sprinkling of clean yellow sand bordering the verges, showed no traces of blood or spent cartridge cases as did most of the village streets. What were the risks in spending the night here in this house? There was plenty of wine, bread, cheese and probably more food in the cellar which he hadn't had the energy to investigate. Should he? Should he take a chance? A weary smile crossed his face as he shook his head. It was one thing to be a sole survivor from a population of six hundred and fifty-three. It was another thing to remain that way!

He stood up unsteadily and picked his way slowly upstairs again, where he took a couple of blankets from a bed in one of the ransacked rooms.

Then, back in the kitchen, he stuffed what remained of the bread and cheese, together with a bottle of red wine, into a string shopping bag. With these things clutched precariously in his good arm and rubbing painfully against his injured one, he went back to the same copse.

Darkness fell quickly into a warm, mellow night with a velvety-blue sky and a three-quarter moon riding serene and uncaring above the scene of carnage. By this time, most of the house fires were dying and it was only above the rooftops that tinges of flame tinged the night sky. In the distance, probably still in the area of the Champ de Foire, he guessed, the Germans continued their celebrations. The officers had clearly given the grenadiers carte-blanche to make the most of the night on their looted drink.

Guerineau wrapped the blankets loosely about him with the uncorked wine at his side. He soon found the blankets made a lot of difference to his comfort, cushioning him against the clumpy grass tufts, easing the pain along his left side. He made no attempt to cover his ears against the German noise; but, eventually, he did manage to clear his mind, isolating himself from the obscenities on all sides and wishing, dear God, that he'd had a detachment of Maquis under his command. As things were, all he could do was try and sleep. He closed his eyes hopefully.

He awoke to the sound of heavy automobile engines revving not very far away. It was daybreak and there was already a hint of the sun edging its yellow rays along the green tops of the yews beyond the copse.

Momentarily he stared about him, disorientated; but then he placed the vehicles in the street alongside the doctor's house. That caused him to sit up. Thank Christ he hadn't taken a chance and slept there!

Several minutes passed before he stirred again and then he threw the blankets from him, surprised to find they were more or less as he'd wrapped them round himself the previous evening – which indicated that he must have had a reasonably restful night. Certainly, he couldn't recall waking.

Now, it appeared, the SS were pulling out of St-Honor. He sipped some of the wine from the bottle and lay back again, listening.

The commands of the SS NCOs grew more vociferous. He also heard the sounds of tailgate chains being released and the clash of metal upon metal as crated automatic weapons and ammunition boxes were thrown aboard. Finally, the heavy clomp of jackboots over the steel-lined floors of the trans-porters as the men climbed aloft.

He glanced at his watch.

Six-fifteen!

As he'd guessed, the SS were making an early start. There were two obvious reasons for this: they needed to be clear of the village before tradesmen and people from Aumont and other neighbouring hamlets came visiting, unaware of the massacre; and, more important, they didn't want to risk contact with any Maquis *réseaux* which might have suspected what had been happening in St-Honor and come to investigate.

More engines started up. The high-revving notes of the scout cars; the deep-throated roar of the powerful Mercedes-Benz staff car. It was simple enough to assimilate these sounds over such a short distance. More raucous commands from more NCOs. A whistle blew and the engine notes intensified. There followed the crunch of tyres over loose aggregate as they pulled away.

Guerineau remained in his prone position, visualising the same German SS who'd committed yesterday's atrocities now sitting calmly in their transporters, most of them nursing thick heads after their night of free liquor. He wondered what could be passing through their minds as they drove past the silent scenes of their devastation and murder.

He let a good half-hour go by before he left the copse, then headed back across the stretch of grass to the doctor's house. As he climbed the steps to the surgery it became apparent that the SS had been here again, too. Now the house was in turmoil and it looked as though they'd had a final root through the household belongings before driving off. He went down into the cellar, seeking food, but it had also been stripped bare. Only a broken wine bottle at the foot of the stone steps suggested that food had been stored here.

Out in the street, the marks of heavy tyres along the sandy verges confirmed his hunch that it was here the SS transport had formed up before leaving. He set off down the lane, past three gutted houses, turning left about forty metres farther along. Presently, he turned left again, to head back parallel to the lane with the eaves of the doctor's house poking above its gutted neighbours, also now on his left.

It was only then that he realised his subconscious had been guiding him back to the garage. Ahead he could see the farm machinery and the flat-cart still littering the road, but the two cars had disappeared. It could be that the SS had taken them, or that they'd merely pushed them down the hill into the river.

As he drew closer to the garage he found his heart quickening, not so much because of his own brush with death there but, more so, because the body of his friend and comrade, Marius Combin, still lay amongst the pile of dead. He should probably drag it clear and find a sheet from somewhere to drape over it. He pondered on that looking through the open door of the workshop, his footsteps getting slower, hesitant even. But when he reached the entrance he knew there was nothing he could do, for the SS had been back there, too. More fires had been started and most of the inside of the workshop was gutted. Almost all the rafters had burned away and dropped on to the corpses beneath. All that now remained was a macabre mix of charred timber and brittle pieces of blackened human flesh, and skulls in which the teeth of the upper jaws appeared startlingly white below the gaping eyesockets.

Guerineau turned away. No way could he search amongst that; the stench of it was making him reel even at a distance of ten metres. The Marius Combin who lay rotting amongst that heap of putrefaction wasn't the same, brave, tireless and dedicated Marius Combin he'd known and loved as a brother. That Marius had gone for all time.

He moved out into the centre of the pavement, staring farther along the street towards the village centre where the buildings were more congested. They looked forlorn and silent, most of them reduced to rubble with thin eddies of grey smoke still curling up from the débris. His plan had been to seek food and wine, but his appetite had disappeared. The all-pervading acrid smell of burning and the sickly-sweet, cloying stench of death was all around him, as bitter as vomit in this throat, clogging his nostrils. Ahead was another pile of bodies and, as he closed the angle, he read the sign above the workshop from which they had spilled: Martin Guilbaud – Forgeron. So this was the location of one more SS execution centre; a smithy and the scene of sixty or seventy more murders!

He halted, again hesitant. In his present physical condition and mental state he'd go out of his mind if he continued making these horrific finds. He had to get out of this dead village as quickly as he could. He'd have telephoned Batiste Couecou or François Herbin at Viverois to come and fetch him if the SS hadn't been smart enough to have torn down the telegraph wires – and what a crisis that would have caused amongst the *réseau*!

Nor were there any cars or even cycles about. If he wanted to get out right now, then he'd have to walk. The only alternative was to hang on until some unsuspecting tradesmen drove into the village intending to start a normal day's work.

Could he face that? Could he stay here to answer the thousand questions they'd throw at him in their horror? Could he help lessen their trepidation at what they were seeing with their own eyes but not believing? He doubted it. He had to go and go now!

He'd contact Couecou later – as soon as he found a telephone which was still functioning – and let the *réseau* take it from there. And they'd waste no time! They'd lynch every one of the bastards who'd been responsible for St-Honor if they had to chase them all the way to Normandy. They'd shadow that SS-grenadier convoy hour by hour, minute by minute. At least Guerineau had the satisfaction of knowing that much. Those SS maniacs had earned themselves deaths far more awesome than those they'd inflicted on the innocent villagers of St-Honor!

He hurried past a doorway in which the body of an elderly woman lay on its back, sprawling over the threshold with the head upside-down three steps lower. She had died either from a stroke or some epileptic fit, for her face was screwed into a gargoyle mask. Her mouth was wide open and crawling with flies. This house was untouched by fire and Guerineau wondered if even the SS had shied from shifting this hideous corpse to get inside. That would have been ironic, for she'd died neither from bullet nor bayonet!

A short distance farther along a group of four teenagers had been murdered together in a small garden at the end of a cul-de-sac where they had evidently found themselves walled in and their escape route cut. There were two slim, blonde girls lying face down amongst a row of tomato plants with their long hair blowing across their faces. Closer to the street lay the bodies of their boyfriends. They were spreadeagled flat on their faces with hands clawing out in front of them, as though they might have made a brave attempt to get at the SS before they'd been gunned down.

Guerineau turned away. He'd just been telling himself to get out of this village. Such chilling finds at every turn were doing him no good at all . . .

He stiffened suddenly in his tracks, listening, before taking a couple of rapid paces into the nearest doorway. It wasn't a good place to seek cover, little more than the four walls of a gutted building which had been a shop of some sort. But he crunched over the charred wood, sinking up to his ankles, jamming the handkerchief over his nostrils, realising there must also be bodies buried here.

Footsteps!

People were coming this way, but he couldn't tell how many for the echoes rang loudly from the pavement, reverberating into the roofless shells of the houses which acted as sound-boxes. Heavy boots! More SS? Not after all he'd been through, for Christ's sake! Why should the SS want to leave an isolated detachment here, anyway?

His reason told him his fears didn't make sense but, all the same, as the footsteps drew closer he moved deeper into the building.

Slowly, as the seconds passed, some of the tension slipped from his face, for he was able to identify only one person. One more survivor? Just one more who'd miraculously survived the carnage? Instant relief flooded his mind, replacing the near-panic of a moment earlier. If this were a villager, then he or she would probably know where to find some form of transport!

On a sudden impulse he stepped out on to the pavement, knowing that if he left his move too late he'd stand a chance of getting himself shot. If whoever it was had survived this much, then they wouldn't be taking any chances now!

'Comrade! Comrade!' Guerineau lifted his good arm high above his head, shouting at the top of his voice. 'Comrade!'

It was a middle-aged man who halted abruptly, panic evident in his face even at a distance of thirty metres. He appeared to be on the point of turning round and running back

135

the way he had come.

'Please!' Guerineau called again, trying to fix a smile on his face, stretching out his right hand in a gesture of friendship. 'Hold it! Please!'

The man was wearing a white jacket with a sweat rag hanging loosely about his neck. Both were filthy, as were his hands and face, but it was clear that he'd been a baker. He still looked unsure of himself, but he didn't run as Guerineau had feared he might, instead he cowered against the wall of the house, trembling, face ashen and mouth working spasmodically.

Guerineau took his time approaching him. As he drew closer he noticed tears running freely through the grime on the man's face.

'My *boulangerie* is full of dead people, *m'sieu*!' he said and there was a plaintive, immature note to his voice which might well have belonged to a child who'd had its favourite toy unaccountably snatched away. 'My ovens are full of bones. They've burned people in my bread ovens, *m'sieu*!'

Guerineau swallowed hard and replied, 'But you're all right, now! You've nothing more to fear. See!' He pointed to the bloody bandages about his left arm. 'The SS shot me, too, but now they've left the village. We're safe, now!'

'But my *boulangerie*! It's crowded with dead people!'

'Yes! Yes! I understand.' Guerineau put his good arm about the man's shoulders and turned him around to head back the way he had come. 'We must go, too, my friend! We must find a telephone and get help.'

The man looked up at him. He was a little fellow with the usual swarthy features of the region, a thick drooping moustache and beetling eyebrows.

He'd been quite strong, Guerineau thought, until the SS had knocked his mind sideways.

'What's your name?' Guerineau asked.

The man hesitated, but then he answered, 'I am Guy Laporte, the village baker . . .' He brushed away tears from his cheeks. 'Do you know I've just seen Louise Boisard?' His face brightened as he spoke the name. 'I have! Really! Dear Louise!'

Guerineau immediately feigned interest, at last hoping to get news of the women and children whom he believed to have been taken to the church. He was about to ask him where he'd seen this woman, but Laporte rushed on before he could get a word in, still in his child's voice. 'You know she was working with me in the Champ de Foire when the SS arrived. She owns the *pâtissèrie*, of course, and we were preparing food for the children's sports . . . and now I have seen her again.' He smiled. 'Not only that, but I touched her cheek! I put out my finger, like this, and do you know it went straight through to the bone? Then Louise just rolled over and her head fell away from her body . . .'

'Where?'

Guerineau hurled the word at him, at the same time grabbing the front of his jacket. 'Where, for Christ's sake? Where did you see this woman?'

Laporte pointed along the street to where the squat tower of the church reached above a sea of green leaves.

Guerineau shook his head violently, unwilling to believe. 'No! Dear God, no! Even the SS wouldn't murder three hundred women and kids!'

Laporte was grinning inanely now, no longer rational. 'I tell you I poked my finger through her cheek and her head fell off!' His voice hardened aggressively. 'If you won't believe me, then go and see for yourself. They're all there! All of 'em!'

'You come with me! Show me where!'

Laporte shook his head, once more cowering against the wall with fresh tears starting.

Guerineau looked up at the church as he'd done a score of times since the SS had left the village. From down here there were no signs of burning, nor of scorched trees around it. He said again, 'Come! Show me!' And, even as he spoke, he wasn't sure whether he was doubting what the man had told him or whether he was shying away from the horrors he might find in that tiny village church. He reached to take the other's arm, but before he could touch him, Laporte swung away and raced down the street howling like a wounded dog.

Guerineau let him go, heading directly towards the church, trying to ignore the scores of mutilated bodies which lay about the streets and in the blackened husks of the houses. It was only when he changed direction to climb a flight of stone steps alongside an escarpment of yellow outcrop that he unexpectedly came down wind of the tower.

The sudden shock caused him clamp his handerchief over his nose. He knew now that Guy Laporte hadn't been raving. If the man were crazy, then it was the scene he'd witnessed here in this church which had turned his mind, not what had gone before!

Momentarily he paused in indecision, considering whether to turn round and head for Aumont whilst he still had his life and his reason. But, seconds later, he resumed his climb. He couldn't ignore this final evidence of the inhumanity of the German SS. He'd come too far, already. He'd got to see it through to the end.

He reached a narrow path which skirted the church, stepping over heaps of spent cartridge cases; both 9mm Schmeiser ammunition and the heavier calibre 7·92mm MG-42 Spandau machine gun. It looked as though there'd been a full-scale battle here, though he knew all of the rounds to have been fired by one side. There were bullet scars round most of the windows, the stained glass shattered, the ancient stonework pitted and pockmarked. Several were also browned with dried blood which had flowed copiously over the sills and dripped into the vegetation below.

The stench became overpowering, reawakening vague sensations of yesterday's nausea. He pressed the handerchief still tighter over his face and continued to the western end of the building where he found one of the high, studded oak doors partly open. Evidently, Guy Laporte had been the first to come here since the SS had left. He peered into the darkness beyond, the stench and the still rising acrid fumes from the charred timber bringing tears to his eyes which he could do nothing about. But, as they grew accustomed to the half-light he could make out the headless body of a woman lying across the nave not a couple of metres in front of him. The rest of the body was burned and blackened with the legs broken and twisted up behind it, whilst scattered around were the charred fragments of the blue and white striped pinafore of the *pâtissière*. So this was all that remained of Louise Boisard! The woman whom her friend, the baker, had touched on the cheek to see her whole face disintegrate. It was this one corpse out of so many which had taken his reason.

He looked over to the eastern transept where a shaft of sunlight speared into the darkness through the open sockets of the shattered windows. It spread in a yellow pool of brightness over the bodies of thirty or more small children who had evidently been grouped there by their mothers to escape the SS

138

during their first brutal sorties amongst them. They were riddled with bullets, their blood dried over the chancel steps, their small limbs blackened by smoke and fire. To their right were a number of prams, also bullet-riddled, whilst lower down at the foot of the altar steps was the body of a small boy shot in an attitude of prayer. In the wooden confessional in the right transept were the bodies of two more women, burned beyond recognition and still holding in their arms the scarred, stick-like creatures which had been their babies.

Guerineau turned away. He'd seen enough! He went out into the sunshine wanting only to hasten his escape. He'd never have believed what his eyes had just confirmed. But for the chance meeting with Guy Laporte he'd have left St-Honor convinced that the women were safe and well either still in the church or in the woods where, initially, he believed the SS had herded them. For several seconds more he stared into the stinking heaps of human remains and then quietly closed the door behind him.

He was a good four kilometres along the Aumont road when he heard the sound of an automobile approaching. Instantly, he froze, moving instinctively into the hedgerow, though this did not have to be the SS. The people of Aumont were still alive and would be beginning their day.

Only those of St-Honor had perished. It had been a mere eighteen hours earlier . . . incredibly, only eighteen hours since they, too, had been going about their village chores and looking forward to the afternoon's festivities.

He peered through the bushes, staring warily down the long, straight road and, immediately, his heart leapt. This was no German staff car, but an ancient Renault which bounced and clattered over the heat ripples in the road surface, its intermittent exhaust note telling of old and irreparable ignition problems.

Guerineau's brow cleared and a smile broke the brittle harshness of his face.

At long last, here was an end to the nightmare.

He stepped out boldly into the centre of the road, aware for the first time that morning of the fair wind of France blowing clean against his face.

Chapter Five

General Friedel von Sahlenburg looked out of his office window high in the city-centre block with his forehead puckered into a frown, his mouth harsh and tight-lipped. It was raining and a dank mist hung over the Loire valley and trailed through the streets like a vague, opaque streamer. Here and there, where it thinned, he could gaze down upon the pavements and watch shabbily dressed French civilians nipping out of the paths of SS and Wehrmacht officers, snug and dry in belted leather coats and mackintoshes. At least the French had learned so much, he told himself: they knew how to make way for their German masters! But then, he reflected, they didn't always move so quickly after dark. There'd been several instances recently when they'd bundled officers off the kerb and scampered away before they could get a second look at them.

But it was neither the weather nor the attitude of the citizens of St Etienne which was worrying the regional commander of Oberkommando Wehrmacht. There were two other things foremost in his mind.

Firstly, he'd just had bad news from the Normandy battlefront. Incredibly bad! So bad that he'd seriously suspected Allied Intelligence of tapping Wehrmacht communications and feeding unadulterated propaganda through the network. Now, he knew he'd been wrong because he'd had the time to back-check. The news was not only bad; it was also correct!

The United States 3rd Army had looped south to Le Mans and then swung back north towards Alencon and Argentan, where it was striving to link up with British and Canadian divisions hammering their way down from the north. Already a pocket was beginning to form between Falaise and Argentan. In addition, the German forces, weakened by non-stop battle involvement since the June landings, were now being subjected to unrestrained bombardment by Allied heavy and fighter-bombers which ran sorties twenty-four hours round the clock. Some crack SS divisions were reported to have been reduced to isolated groups of battalion and company strength and to be clinging desperately to the few crossings over the Dives river, whilst more Allied squadrons moved farther east to destroy bridges over the Seine and halt German reinforcements in troops and armour bound for the battlefront. Indications were, the communique read, that the German 5th and 7th Armies could be isolated within the Falaise pocket unless something like a miracle happened. German losses since the Allied landings topped 300,000 and a further 100,000 casualties were anticipated during this crucial battle for Normandy.

So von Sahlenburg, with ripe personal memories of Kharkov and Dnepropetrovsk etched indelibly into his mind, had cause to be worried at the possibility of an equally devastating defeat here, not a couple of hundred kilometres north of this very office!

Secondly, and equally important as far as he was concerned, trouble was arising from the Uber Alles involvement at St-Honor a couple of days ago. Number 2 Company of the 2nd Panzergrenadier Battalion was back in billets in St Etienne, awaiting movement orders which, in turn, were dependent on an accurate definition of the extent of the American breakthrough. In fact, the SS were here on his doorstep when he'd have wished them in hell. Bloody fools! They could have got away with chopping up the men. They could have been rigged on Maquis collaboration charges and the executions legalised under the irregular terrorist plan – as at Talmont-les-deux-Ponts. There, the French peasants hadn't liked seeing hostages being shot either, but they'd bloody well had to lump it! What else could they expect when the Maquis had chopped down a hundred soldiers of the 603rd Infantry Battalion?

But not the women and kids! Christ! Not the women and kids!

He hadn't been satisfied either by Bucholz and Schroeder's glib explanation that they'd given orders to young Odermatt to take the women and children into the woods and that he'd locked them in the church on his own authority and burned them alive there! Burned them alive! Jesus Christ! Even the Gestapo wouldn't have burned alive three hundred women and kids! But his two aides had watched that happen and Bucholz had been in command on seniority, no matter how he tried to involve Untersturmfuhrer Werner Odermatt!

What niggled him, too, was a sneaky fear that they were

prepared to under-rate his intelligence – an old man secure in his desk job two hundred kilometres from the bullets and shrapnel and determined to stay there at all costs. That could hurt, especially when he'd moved heaven and earth to get them here!

And now Monseigneur de Michele, Bishop of St Etienne, had written an incredulous letter to General Rudiger Schellinger, Commanding the St Etienne Feldgendarmerie and Militia, claiming that the tabernacle at St-Honor had been forced and the sacred vessels stolen. The wanton murder of the women and children was unbelievable. Unbelievable! The bishop had wept and prayed ever since he'd heard the news.

The general, an elderly Wehrmacht officer of the Prussian Cavalry School, had known nothing either of the pillaging of St-Honor or of the genocide there until he received the bishop's letter when, equally shocked, he had promised the bishop there would be an immediate investigation.

Von Sahlenburg had not been happy, either, at the general's persistence and had stressed the point that the SS were not called upon to report their plans or duties to the Wehrmacht, but . . .! But the executions had been essential because a council order had been received direct from Generalfeldmarschall Keitel to put an end to localised Maquis action against the SS immediately. The Maquis had taken German lives at Talmont-les-deux-Ponts and also at St-Honor, as they had at many other towns in the Zone. It had also been the Maquis who were directly responsible for the bombing of the two panzergrenadier regiments in the Fôret d'Ivres, south of Vichy.

What was he supposed to do, General Schellinger? Sit on his arse? After Keitel had telephoned him from Normandy, personally? And, as for the women and children . . . well! That had been a most unfortunate accident! They'd been locked in the church to keep them out of harm's way, but the sparks from other fires in the village had set the place alight. Unfortunately, too, Maquis explosives had been stored behind the altar and beneath the vestry floor and the heat from the fire had detonated these. The SS had done their damnedest to get the women and children out, but they'd been beaten back by the flames. That's how it was. There was no need for any kind of a court of inquiry. He would be compiling a comprehensive report for the Generalfeldmarschall and would ensure that an edited copy was also sent to Monseigneur the Bishop. Would the general be kind enough, therefore, to pass that information on to the bishop at his first opportunity?

That had got the genocide at St-Honor off his back for the time being, but probably only for the time being. After Bucholz and Schroeder's denial of any personal orders concerning the plight of the women and children, he'd sent a platoon back to St-Honor under the command of Untersturmfuhrer Wolfgang Sieloff with orders to tidy up the mess and make sure the French didn't start drifting in from surrounding villages until they'd had a chance to do so. That had resulted in Number 2 Company being retained in St Etienne longer than he had anticipated. Furthermore, little had been achieved in St-Honor, for he'd since learned that civilians *had* been moving in and out of the village, even during the night of the SS occupation!

He also had doubts concerning the suitability of Sieloff. The untersturmfuhrer appeared to have sympathies towards the French. Goddammit! An SS officer! There'd been distinct aggression in his tone when he'd reported that irrefutable evidence indicated that when they'd found their asphyxiation plan in the church wasn't going to work, Odermatt's grenadiers had fired low into the women and children. Some of the bodies had had their legs shot away and, as a result, these people could only have been burned alive. Not even the babies had been spared! Sieloff reported finding prams unreached by the flames, but riddled with bullets. The corpse of a child had even been found dumped head first in the font!

Similar atrocities were in evidence all around the village. Sieloff reported finding the bodies of invalids murdered where they lay with their medicines and sickroom paraphernalia still littering their bedside tables. Bodies were clogging up the well in the Champ de Foire, and corpses had been piled over the forge at the smithy where they'd been shrivelled to cinders.

Despite von Sahlenburg's dislike of Sieloff, he knew there was no reason for him to believe that the officer was doing anything other than speaking the truth. There were no reasons why he should, or should want to fabricate such statements. Besides, it would be a simple matter to seek collaborative statements from NCOs.

But one thing was certain – it was impossible for the SS to cover up their tracks! This off-the-record report he'd just made to General Rudiger Schellinger would have to suffice until he'd briefed Bucholz and Schroeder accordingly. In the meantime, he'd pull all the strings he could to have Number 2 Panzergrenadier Company shifted north without delay. An important point was that whilst it would be the easiest thing in the world to make young Odermatt the scapegoat, no way could he risk him facing a court-martial!

The war news which had come like the kick of a mule to General Friedel von Sahlenburg reached the hard-pressed French population as a breath of heaven – by way of the British Broadcasting Corporation's service to occupied countries.

Furthermore, Allied reports had been as optimistic as German communiques to their General Staff had been guarded. Also, to convince the citizens of St Etienne that this was no ambitious piece of Allied propaganda, telephone calls had been received from friends and relations in Normandy who had already been liberated by triumphant British, Canadian and American armies.

Some – a few – had had their property devastated in the action, but others had escaped without damage or personal injury and were now busy tidying their gardens! Still more, whose voices had been barely articulate through their tears, had seen the reconnaissance spearhead of the American 3rd Army – the 2nd Free French Armoured Division, chasing along the roads after the fleeing panzers, with their tricolour pennants flying and the Cross of Lorraine emblazoned on the sides of their Shermans and scout cars. Probably that, more than anything else, had put the people of St Etienne in a kind of mood which neither the threats of Oberkommando Wehrmacht and its Feldgendarmerie and Militia jackals, nor the prospects of a blustery and stormy day, could do anything to lessen.

It was about 11.30 am when the 1·5 litre Citroen with young François Herbin at the wheel turned into the northern suburbs of St Etienne. At his side, hunched in the passenger seat, was Armand Guerineau.

Guerineau was desperately ill and looked it. His normally chubby and ruddy face was pinched and yellow, the pain evident in his eyes. Gangrene had manifested itself in his elbow wound. Clearly, his forty-eight hour wait for professional medical attention, the bacteria contained within the richly fertilised soil of St-Honor and the sapping of his strength during the SS occupation had all taken their toll.

He had been aware of the gangrene before he was taken to Dr Georges Bousquier's surgery, but had seemingly attached little importance to it. That had puzzled François Herbin and Batiste Couecou who had both seen other members of the *réseau* die from similar infections. So why was Armand treating his own wound so lightly?

Georges Bousquier took swabs which he analysed in a tiny laboratory attached to his surgery. When he reappeared he gave the news to Guerineau straight.

'It's bad, Armand.' There was a brisk efficiency in his tone which belied the anxiety in his eyes and the creases in his forehead. 'The fact is I'll have to amputate the arm and now! I mean, right now!' He turned on impulse, glancing back pensively towards the open door of his laboratory. 'Problem is, I've so very few drugs and barely any anaesthetics. It's going to hurt like hell, but you'll have to make out with cognac. The important thing is to get the arm off before the infection spreads through the body. You understand, of course?'

Guerineau nodded wearily.

'I understand, Georges. But I don't agree!'

'Don't agree?' A faint smile touched the doctor's mouth and contrasted with the worry-lines about his face. 'Don't agree?' he echoed, looking from Couecou to Herbin as though he hadn't heard correctly. 'But you're acquainted with gangrene, Armand! You, too, have seen people die as we all have. Are you telling me it can't happen to you? For, believe me, it can and will unless I amputate!'

'It means I've got other things to do!'

'What kind of other things, for God's sake? What can be more important than your survival? To yourself! To Françoise and the kids! To the *réseau*, goddammit! The Franc Tireurs et Partisans can't shrug off its leaders as recklessly as that, Armand.' He turned again to the others, appealing to them to recognise his logic, even if their leader had his priorities mixed up. But then he swung back to Guerineau as a new thought struck him. He said, 'It's not that . . . that . . . you've a thing about this kind of an operation, is it Armand? For I've known men as brave as you shy at losing a limb. But you'll be all right in a couple of weeks. The arm's already gone. It's dead flesh. Dead! It's a corpse all of its own, and unless we take it away from the clean part of your body, then that will die, too. There's no chance of saving the arm. None! But it's your left, isn't it? You're not going to be a cripple!'

Again Guerineau shook his head.

'When I said I didn't agree just now, Georges, I didn't mean I didn't agree with your diagnosis. So all right! There's gangrene in my left arm. Like you say, I've seen it happen to others in the *réseau* and I accept that it's now happened to me. Take my word for it, you'd know just how much I accept it if you were at my end of the pain! But what I'm saying is that you can't take it off right now. Not this afternoon!'

'Armand! Every minute we delay increases the risk of the infection spreading. It's doing so even as we talk, the only thing we don't know is how quickly. A few more hours may be too late!'

'I need twenty-four hours.'

'Impossible!'

'It's a chance I've got to take!'

'No!'

Guerineau turned to Couecou and Herbin. 'Get me out of here, you two! The man won't listen.'

But even they hesitated, looking from Guerineau to the doctor with worried expressions. It crossed Couecou's mind that had Bousquier had the opportunity he'd have clubbed Guerineau there and then and got on with the operation, feeding him anaesthetics as and when he showed signs of coming round.

Bousquier tried a new tack.

'What is it you have to do, Armand? At least you can tell me that!'

But Guerineau shook his head.

'No! I can't even tell you that, Georges, apart from that it's something personal.'

'For the *réseau*?'

'Mainly for me.'

So, now, eighteen hours later, Guerineau was slumped in the front seat of the Citroen with François Herbin at the wheel, heading through driving rain towards the city centre.

Batiste Couecou had taken up a dog-watch on the infants' school in which the Number 2 Panzergrenadier Company were still billeted. He also had a car standing by equipped with short-wave radio. His job was to tail the SS convoy when it left

146

St Etienne and radio its position ahead to detached *réseaux* of the Franc Tireurs et Partisans. So far, things had worked out well. The next few hours would test the ingenuity of the pre-planning.

That morning there were few people about in the city. It was unlikely that this was due to a worsening of the weather, but rather because they were too excited by the war news to go about their usual shopping routine; preferring, instead, to drop into neighbours' homes or street café-bars to speculate upon the chances of a speedy German defeat. The few who were about dashed across the roads with heads deep in the collars of their mackintoshes, frequently being compelled to scurry out of the way of Wehrmacht service trucks, which splashed and jolted through the built-up area at their usual breakneck speed as though the whole German war effort depended on the time it took them to get to the industrial estate where most of their composite rations were stored. It was as the Citroen drew level with the tall municipal office block which housed the Regional Headquarters of Oberkommando Wehrmacht that the engine began to splutter, alternately misfiring and spitting back through the carburettor and then belching black smoke in a sudden fierce blast as mixture exploded in the silencer. The car shuddered to a halt.

At once, Herbin jumped out, dragging his mackintosh loosely about his head and shoulders against the heavy rain, then springing open the bonnet and peering beneath. His fingers moved expertly over the ignition system and when he straightened up he was holding a cracked distributor cap with its four plug leads trailing for Guerineau to see. He shrugged helplessly into the open window and then turned to hurry across the square with the distributor cap still hanging from his hand.

Guerineau sank back into his seat with a great sigh. Without the clatter of the worn engine and the swish of bald tyres through the puddles, the rain seemed to be beating all the harder on the metal top of the car. The windshield was already misting and the bonnet, still raised, cut off most of his vision to the front. To his left was the Oberkommando Wehrmacht office block. To his right, across the square, was the Café Au Moulin de Vent, into which he watched the slim figure of François Herbin disappear.

So all he could do now was wait.

And he hadn't long to wait — about four minutes.

Then, as though on cue, a couple of feldgendarmes wearing steel helmets, mackintoshes and carrying G-41 (M) self-loading rifles came running down the steps to the road. Their heads were bent against the driving rain, but there was no doubt where they were heading. They halted beside Guerineau's Citroen, breathing heavily, stooping and craning their necks to look inside.

Guerineau wound down his window.

The leading feldgendarme spoke harshly, at the same time pointing up at the office building as though he might be being watched by some higher authority.

'You can't park here!' he bellowed above the rattle of the rain on the car roof, his guttural French as nauseating to Guerineau as only Germans could make it. 'These are military premises. No parking! So move on!'

Guerineau smiled helplessly.

'I wish I could, officer,' he said evenly, 'but, unfortunately, the distributor cap has cracked and the rain seeped into the ignition.' He shrugged. 'My friend has gone to get a replacement. There are plenty about for this model, I believe. He will be no more than a few minutes.'

'You can't stay here!'

'Only a few minutes!'

The feldgendarme bridled.

'Not even a few bloody seconds! Don't you hear what I say? These are military premises. No one is allowed to park here!'

'But what can I do? The car won't run without a distributor cap.'

'You can get out and shove it across the road!'

Guerineau smiled wanly as he shook his head.

'But look at me, officer,' he reasoned quietly. 'Just look at me! Do you think I'm capable of pushing an automobile? I was on my way to hospital for urgent treatment. That's where my friend was taking me now. Because I'm not fit enough to use public transport.'

The German hesitated, staring into Guerineau's haggard and pallid face. There was no doubt that this man was ill. Desperately ill! Guerineau saw his expression change and when he took his head out from inside the car to seek his companion's opinion, he breathed a sigh of relief.

When they had gone, Guerineau sank back into his seat with

eyes turned up to the grey sky, the shafts of rain like silver rods against the red brick of the tall building. To his left, the opaque windows gazed down upon him like so many silent watchers and he wondered who might be up there and who'd seen the feldgendarmes at his car. Not that it mattered a damn! He'd never thought for a minute they'd bend their own backs to shove it across the street. The best they could have hoped for was to grab a few passers-by and ordered them to do it. But there'd been no passers-by. At least he could thank the rain for that!

At the top of the steps the feldgendarmes had halted to turn back to him. One of them made the gesture of pointing at his wristwatch. Guerineau nodded and raised a hand in acknowledgement. Yes. He'd be on his way as soon as he could manage it. But then he glanced at his own watch. Fifteen minutes to noon!

Christ! So close?

Sturmbannfuhrer Kurt Bucholz and Hauptsturmfuhrer Jurgen Schroeder opened the door into General Friedel von Sahlenburg's office at his command. They halted a couple of metres apart and saluted together as though they had long practiced the drill.

'Yes! Yes! Yes!'

The general acknowledged them testily with a lift of a hand, looking up from his desk and scowling. He'd had a growing suspicion that morning that perhaps he might have been a little too impulsive in clamouring at HQ for the posting of these two young officers to St Etienne. During the past twenty-four hours in particular, he'd experienced considerable disillusionment, for there was little doubt that since they'd been taken from the fighting front they'd got the idea they were on some sort of extended furlough, during which they could do whatever they liked and when they liked without criticism or restraint.

That was a fair assessment, von Sahlenburg told himself now as he looked over their tall, athletic figures, their immaculate uniforms bearing the cuff and epaulette insignia of the Uber Alles Division and Iron Crosses, Classes 1 and 2. They were too bloody perfect! They'd too much conceit about their own past glories. More than that, they knew that the worst thing he could do to them was return them to the division which, the general admitted, was probably just what they were seeking! Could be that the lack of conformity was due to nothing other than boredom. Boredom in St Etienne! He'd never considered that when he'd secured their appointment. But now, in retrospect, it made a lot of sense. That was probably why they'd made such a meal of the reprisals at St-Honor — because they'd been bloody bored! They'd seized that one and only chance to hurl themselves back into the cut and thrust of the Waffen SS. Hanging the blame on to young Odermatt had probably been their idea of a joke.

'Look! Both of you!' Von Sahlenburg cleared his throat noisily. 'We can't just shrug off this St-Honor incident. Already there are repercussions from the local clergy, from the Wehrmacht General Staff and, no doubt, there are more on their way from HQ. I need a comprehensive report from both of you and quickly.'

'But of course, sir!' Bucholz replied easily. 'Though you must appreciate that we can only put into writing a report identical to that we have given you verbally.' He paused, smiling. 'Perhaps I should also repeat that if you also intend to obtain a report from Untersturmfuhrer Werner Odermatt, he will undoubtedly deny having received my orders to lead the women and children of St-Honor into the woods during the period of the execution of the males. That, I suppose, will be his defence, though we all know that the killing went to his head and that he burned the women and children in the church!'

He glanced at Schroeder who sensed the movement and nodded gravely without turning his head.

'Yes! Yes! Yes!' The irritation had not left the general's tone. He pushed back his chair and stood up, then glanced at his wristwatch and immediately busied himself in collecting together the loose papers spread haphazardly across his desk. He bundled them into a leather briefcase. 'Yes! That's what I expected you to say.' He shrugged. 'Not that I've any cause to doubt your word, of course! So Odermatt lost his self-control? Fair enough. I've seen that happen, too, but the problem is that the generalfeldmarschall not only gave us a carte-blanche to handle St-Honor, but he also provided the SS company to do it!'

'It's quite a simple story really, sir. The execution of the men was necessary because of the bombing in the Fôret d'Ivres laager which, itself, was a backlash following the SS involvement at Talmont. As a result of that bombing and a personal commitment in the fighting, young Odermatt temporarily lost his self-control.' Schroeder spread out his hands as he finished speaking. As he'd claimed, this was a simple story, uncomplicated, and could well be true.

'But that's only correct so far as it goes, Jurgen,' Von Sahlenburg's doubt was reflected in his voice as he pulled on his mackintosh. 'There are questions which will have to be answered. Keitel's staff aren't bloody fools, you know, even if they've got a war on their hands. They'll want a full statement for Berlin, just in case . . .' At that point he stopped struggling into the sleeves and eyed the two young officers dispassionately . . . 'just in case things get worse in Normandy and somebody, someday, has to explain exactly what did happen in St-Honor!' Bucholz reacted immediately, but von Sahlenburg waved him into silence, adding; 'Don't be too much the SS commander, Kurt! For God's sake, you've read the bulletin this morning. It's not impossible that the Yanks could close the gap at Falaise!'

'Then, sir,' Schroeder put in in a calm, reasoning voice, 'what would you like us to do?'

Von Sahlenburg grabbed the briefcase from the desk.

'We compile a statement without delay. I've got Keitel's original council order here concerning reprisals against French civilians, together with all subsequent relevant orders, telephone conversations and Gestapo reports. We shall take these to the mess and, over lunch, decide upon a positive line of action. All right?'

Down in the foyer the guard commander was quick to jab at a bellpush and, as the trio approached, the grenadiers at either side of the door snapped into a copybook present arms. Von Sahlenburg acknowledged absently, pausing on the top step to scowl upon the misty, rain-drenched square. There were few people about and he wasn't surprised for the day looked more like autumn than mid-summer.

A Wehrmacht truck splashed by, cascading spray over an old Citroen saloon parked haphazardly against the kerb with its bonnet raised. There was no sign of the driver and he guessed the deluge had washed that out, too. He glanced at his companions who shrugged their acceptance of the bad weather, causing the general to drag his belt tighter about his body as he stepped from under cover.

In the Citroen, Armand Guerineau lay with his head resting in the gap between the passenger's and the driver's seat. In that position he was able to see round the edge of the raised bonnet without being seen from the steps. He was aware that his strength was ebbing fast. The physical demands and the tensions of the occasion were already taking their toll, causing his head to swim in recurring seas of nausea which clouded his vision, sent his heart thumping and his wound throbbing.

When that happened, he hung on staring up at the roof-line of the high building, concentrating his mind on his roadside cottage at Viverois; on his dark-haired wife, Françoise, and their two young children, Yves and Christiane. The kids would be at school right now, whilst he was sitting here dying in this beat-up old car in a square in St Etienne. There was something very sad about it all, he reflected, but at least they'd been spared the torture and killing of St-Honor. Yet the women and children who'd perished there had all been somebody's loved ones, even though the men had themselves died before they could know what the SS had planned to do with their families. That had been something of a blessing.

He sensed movement at the top of the steps and shifted his head slightly to see two SS guards going through a present arms routine. A few seconds later, the portly figure of General Friedel von Sahlenburg appeared in the entrance flanked on either side by a tall young officer.

Guerineau breathed a sigh. He'd never seen these officers before, but he guessed they could only be the newest recruits to the OKW fold — Sturmbannfuhrer Kurt Bucholz and Haupt-sturmfuhrer Jurgen Schroeder. *Mon Dieu*! *Merci*! *Merci*!

Von Sahlenburg hesitated on the top step. It was obvious that the general was looking over at the Citroen, but then he turned to his companions to make some remark or other and began moving down the steps.

Guerineau leaned farther back in his seat. He knew there wasn't a chance in hell of him passing out now. The adrenalin coursing through his veins would keep him conscious just as long as was necessary. Afterwards, it didn't matter a damn! He took his eyes from the trio to dart a quick glance round the square: to the Café Au Moulin de Vent where he knew young François Herbin to be, at the rain bouncing off the pavement in front of a department store which took up the whole of the north side.

A great calm settled over his body. His head was clearing and even his wound had ceased its throbbing. He was going to have sufficient strength when he needed it and that made everything worthwhile. He was desperately sorry for Françoise and the kids, but he'd got no choice. Besides, Georges Bousquier hadn't fooled him one little bit when he'd claimed he could save his life if he'd amputated the arm yesterday afternoon. That had been so much flannel! Old Georges had always had far too cosy a bedside manner – refusing to accept the inevitable until his patient had become a cooling corpse. Long before the doctor had stated his diagnosis, Guerineau had known that the gangrene had spread beyond his arm. With the unavailability of drugs in that part of France there had never been the remotest chance of his survival. No man could survive a wound as infected as his and, in his own mind, he didn't deserve to!

Why?

Because in the final analysis it had been he who'd been indirectly responsible for the massacre that was St-Honor. The easy victory over the inexperienced German 603rd Infantry Battalion at Talmont-les-deux-Ponts should have been the beginning and the end of the Maquis campaign in that part of France.

But he'd gone too far.

There'd been no need to rub the Wehrmacht's nose so hard in the muck! He should have accepted the simple fact that no Maquis guerilla group would be allowed to get away with that degree of humiliation of a German unit – not even the 603rd.

As a result there had followed the predictable chain reaction of reprisal, revenge, more reprisal, more revenge!

A sudden chill enveloped him as his mind flitted back to the scene in the St-Honor church. He knew that, had he survived, those memories would have haunted him for the rest of his life: the half-burned bodies of the women in the wooden confessional, blasted by machine gun bullets and yet still clutching the blackened, stick-like remains of their babies to their bosoms; a small boy slumped on the altar steps in an attitude of prayer with a neat necklace of bullet holes across his back.

St-Honor had been the final link in that chain and, ultimately, he'd been responsible for it all!

What had Oberstleutnant Lothar Overath of the 603rd Infantry Battalion said as he'd stood in surrender that night in

Talmont-les-deux-Ponts beneath the burning shells of the *mairie* and the Auberge de la Bobotte? – 'You win today, my friend! But soon you will lose. And how you will lose! You must know as well as I that Oberkommando Wehrmacht will not tolerate an outrage such as this. The streets of your lovely villages will run red with French blood!'

The significant thing about the speech had been that the colonel hadn't been threatening. He'd merely been stating a fact!

Round the raised bonnet of the Citroen he could glimpse the three SS officers turning towards him from the foot of the steps. Von Sahlenburg was still in the centre of the group and all three were leaning into the weather, slitting their eyes against the sting of the rain.

He watched them approach without moving a muscle. Twenty metres to go! He pushed his right hand under the driver's seat and his fingers grasped the fluted steel barrel of an MP-40 Schmeiser machine pistol. The effort caused his heart to palpitate and for a few desperate seconds his head swam in a new surge of nausea. He tugged again at the Schmeiser, harder, but the magazine had jammed fast behind the metal tubes of the seat supports.

Guerineau's eyes were still fixed on the three SS officers as sweat began to course freely down his forehead. Christ! But he mustn't panic! He didn't know whether this was reaction to the jammed Schmeiser or whether it could be a prelude to an incapacitating nausea which would evaporate what remained of his fast-ebbing strength within seconds. The bloody gun was still wedged beneath the seat! If the trigger caught on the supports he'd probably fire a burst into the fuel tank and fry himself alive . . .

Suddenly it came free and he jerked it across his knees, throwing himself forward so that the weight of his body pressed the gun tighter against his thighs. Please God, Herbin had remembered to cock the gun! That was something he should have checked before the boy left the car!

The forefinger of his right hand had found the trigger and the bolt lever was at the rear of the gun, thank God! The three officers were not more than ten metres away . . . nine! eight! seven! He found himself making a countdown on reflex. The one nearest the kerb was pointing towards the Citroen, probably for the first time realising it was occupied. Guerineau at once reacted to the threat, knowing that the guards at the top of the steps would already have their rifles trained on him, just in case! And, as Jurgen Schroeder stooped to peer inside, Guerineau squeezed the trigger.

The Schmeiser jolted and bucked over his thighs as he blazed through the side of the car. He held his grip doggedly, seeing the officers hurled across the pavement by the force of the fusillade, to slump heavily against a low brick wall which edged the strip of lawn. He was conscious of their blood, immediately thinned by the bouncing rain, coursing in a quick-flowing orange-brown stream across the pavement to the gutter where the swirling water whisked it away. Still he held on to the trigger, watching the lifeless bodies continue to thresh and jump beneath the cone of fire. He saw von Sahlenburg's head suddenly crack open as though he'd been hit by a giant axe. The same burst caught one of the other officers across the throat, severing the jugular vein so that his blood spurted in a crimson fountain to a height of two metres. The magazine emptied and the bodies sank into impossible positions.

Guerineau lifted his eyes to the top of the steps where more soldiers were dashing from the guardroom. He saw the dull, orange muzzle flashes of their rifles and automatic weapons and was even aware of the bullets tearing through the side of the Citroen, matching those drilled by his Schmeiser. As oblivion claimed him, he was thinking it was a bloody shame that the Boches were going to get their gun back!

Across the square at the Café Au Moulin de Vent, young François Herbin crossed himself and quietly left the building through a door at the rear.

Now it was his turn!

Today he, too, had to kill a man.

An SS officer.

Untersturmfuhrer Werner Odermatt — and he knew exactly where to find him!

COLDITZ
by Reinhold Eggers

Colditz. Easily the best-known of all the German P.O.W. prison camps. A fortress where only the most dangerous and incorrigible escapers were confined. The Germans thought it was an excellent idea to try and keep all of their problem prisoners of war in the one jail.

During the latter part of the war the author was in charge of security at the prison and he reveals for the first time from the German side, just how surprising was the result of their plan. The book is both entertaining and exciting. It is one of the finest and must unusual stories to come out of the Second World War.

'By far the best account of this extraordinary camp.' –
Airey Neave, M.P., in the *Sunday Telegraph*

'A must for escapologists. Crammed with the techniques of escaping. I was impressed by the consistent accuracy through the book.' –
P. R. Reid (author of 'Colditz Story') in the *Evening Standard*

'Reveals a profound, unexpected knowledge of British P.O.W. psychology. Will provide great entertainment. More amusing than I thought possible.' –
Douglas Bader in the *News of the World*

NEW ENGLISH LIBRARY

NEL BESTSELLERS

T037061	BLOOD AND MONEY	*Thomas Thompson*	£1.50
T045692	THE BLACK HOLE	*Alan Dean Foster*	95p
T049817	MEMORIES OF ANOTHER DAY	*Harold Robbins*	£1.95
T049701	THE DARK	*James Herbert*	£1.50
T045528	THE STAND	*Stephen King*	£1.75
T065475	I BOUGHT A MOUNTAIN	*Thomas Firbank*	£1.50
T050203	IN THE TEETH OF THE EVIDENCE	*Dorothy L. Sayers*	£1.25
T050777	STRANGER IN A STRANGE LAND	*Robert Heinlein*	£1.75
T050807	79 PARK AVENUE	*Harold Robbins*	£1.75
T042308	DUNE	*Frank Herbert*	£1.50
T045137	THE MOON IS A HARSH MISTRESS	*Robert Heinlein*	£1.25
T050149	THE INHERITORS	*Harold Robbins*	£1.75
T049620	RICH MAN, POOR MAN	*Irwin Shaw*	£1.60
T046710	EDGE 36: TOWN ON TRIAL	*George G. Gilman*	£1.00
T037541	DEVIL'S GUARD	*Robert Elford*	£1.25
T050629	THE RATS	*James Herbert*	£1.25
T050874	CARRIE	*Stephen King*	£1.50
T050610	THE FOG	*James Herbert*	£1.25
T041867	THE MIXED BLESSING	*Helen Van Slyke*	£1.50
T038629	THIN AIR	*Simpson & Burger*	95p
T038602	THE APOCALYPSE	*Jeffrey Konvitz*	95p
T046850	WEB OF EVERYWHERE	*John Brunner*	85p

NEL P.O. BOX 11, FALMOUTH TR10 9EN, CORNWALL

Postage charge:
U.K. Customers. Please allow 40p for the first book, 18p for the second book, 13p for each additional book ordered, to a maximum charge of £1.49, in addition to cover price.

B.F.P.O. & Eire. Please allow 40p for the first book, 18p for the second book, 13p per copy for the next 7 books, thereafter 7p per book, in addition to cover price.

Overseas Customers. Please allow 60p for the first book plus 18p per copy for each additional book, in addition to cover price.

Please send cheque or postal order (no currency).

Name ....

Address ....

....

Title ....

While every effort is made to keep prices steady, it is sometimes necessary to increase prices at short notice. New English Library reserve the right to show on covers and charge new retail prices which may differ from those advertised in the text or elsewhere.(5)